About the Author

Phil Hughes was born in Kingston-Upon-Thames in England. He spent his life travelling, at first as the dependent of a Royal Air Force pharmacist, and then as a contract technical writer. After working as a writer for others for thirty-five years, Phil decided to break away from his comfort zone and attempt a career doing what he loves best, writing fiction.

Archie's Problem is the first book in The Hidden Syndicate series. Gigi's Cause, the second book is planned for issue in the second half of 2017. Izzo's Solution, the third book is planned for issue in the last quarter of the year.

Visit http://www.facebook.com/CamorraChronicles to find out more about the author and his works.

Other books by the same author:

- *Vendetta*

ARCHIE'S PROBLEM

First Published 2017

Amazon ASIN: B06WRV5BH3
Paperback ISBN: 978-0-9956714-2-3

This one is for Sally, whose faith that I would manage to complete the tale in the allotted time was inspirational as well as driving.

Historical Note

The military base at Bagnoli where some of the action of this tale takes place has since been closed down, and the Allied Forces Southern Europe (AFSOUTH) moved to Lago Patria, a little further up the coast. At the time when the story is set, Bagnoli was a buzzing NATO base, although primarily US forces occupied it. The base at Lago Patria was predominately a Royal Air Force base.

If memory serves me correctly, there was only one entrance into the base at Bagnoli, and I have taken the liberty of Archie assuming there were more, although that was not the case.

The incident with the armoured vehicle breaking through the borders of Northern Italy is based on real events, though I have changed the circumstances considerably. The actual event amounted to Neapolitan crime syndicates deciding that cigarette smuggling was a tolerated occupation, but they underestimated the reaction when Italian law enforcement officers lost their lives. It was effectively the end of the contraband cigarette trade around the Naples region, and indeed throughout Italy.

At the time when the story is set, there were helmet laws in Italy, but they were effectively ignored. That too has since changed and wearing of helmets being compulsory is now policed.

Phil Hughes
February 2017

Acknowledgements

Many have assisted me in writing Archie's Problem. Those include John the editing machine who somehow managed to keep me close to the straight and narrow; Sally who read the book and provided me with very insightful feedback, which I took on board; Michelle who also provided me with some useful tips about the content of the tale, which I also took on board and Eoin who provided input after the first draft was completed. Many friends also took the time to read the book and provide a feeling about the readability of it from a reader's viewpoint, rather than an editor's viewpoint.

Thanks to each of you for helping me to complete the book. Your copies are in the post.

I also must thank Google Maps for their Street View, because I have not been back to Naples where the story is set since 2006. It was very useful as a pro-Memoria to look at the streets of the city as they are today.

PHIL

HUGHES

ARCHIE'S

PROBLEM

Contents

Chapter 1

Detective Sergeant Richard Thumper had a problem.

It was not so much that his leg was itching and aching in its cast, although it was, or that he had been standing on it for the last ten minutes in utter silence, although he had. The wait was grating on his nerves and his eighteen stones were grinding on his broken knee. He had known that an interview with Superintendent "Dugs" Douglas would happen. There was no way that the events of the night before would go unchallenged, not with his SO14 colleagues bouncing on the same shift in the club. He had also known that taking on the Roper's gig would lead to trouble, but foolishly tried to convince himself that when it came, the trouble would be directed elsewhere.

The Super was not only pissed off because he had to come to The Yard on a Saturday morning, but also because one of his team had dropped a bollock. That much would have been evident to a small child. Since Thumper entered the office, Dugs had not looked up from the document he was reading. The DS was sure he had heard "Enter" when he knocked on the door, but the Superintendent had not moved since then. He seemed to be frozen in the act of reading the document on his desk.

Thumper's conviction about what he had heard was beginning to waver. He even wondered if Dugs had fallen asleep, or died. His eyes were open, but what did that mean? Thumper knew soldiers who could sleep with their eyes open when they were on sentry duty, so why not Dugs? Also, in his capacity as a police officer he had seen many corpses and they all had their eyes open. Well, one or two corpses, anyway. Okay, one, the old biddy in the flat next door who passed away from a stroke last Christmas, but who's counting?

Perhaps foolishly, he cleared his throat loudly and regretted it immediately, because of the withering look the Super levelled at him.

"What the fuck, Detective? What the fuck!"

"I beg your pardon, sir?"

"Whatever possessed you to be caught in such a predicament?" Thumper shrugged, not knowing how to answer the question.

"Do you know what I am reading, Sergeant?"

"No, sir!"

"Do you think it is a copy of the annual metropolitan police budget report, which I found in the privy when I went for a crap this morning?"

"No, sir!" Thumper guessed the Super had been thinking up the line since he had entered the office.

"No, sir. No, it is not, Sergeant, it is a report of your balls-up in Roper's nightclub." A report that had been brought to the Super's attention by mobile phone as he was tying the laces of his golf shoes in the changing room of the exclusive club for senior police officers. Tying the laces had been in preparation to his foursome with the Assistant Commissioner, Commander Willett and Commander Jones and two of his Superintendent peers in Specialist Operations. He should have been negotiating budgets while playing a leisurely back nine, not carpeting a Detective Sergeant because of gross incompetence. He would have left it to the Chief Inspector to handle, but Bond had been adamant that Dugs handle it himself.

"Yes, sir." Thumper said.

"Ah, finally an affirmative. What the hell were you doing bouncing in a nightclub, anyway?" Thumper remained silent.

"Do you know, Sergeant, what the Metropolitan Police Service policy is regarding moonlighting?"

"Yes, sir."

"Yes, sir? What is it then, Sergeant?"

"It is frowned upon but not forbidden, sir."

"Mm. That is a pretty liberal interpretation of the regulations Sergeant. We do not condone moonlighting, Sergeant. Not in any form, but especially not in a dive like Roper's."

Thumper frowned then. Roper's was possibly the most exclusive nightclub in London, frequented only by the rich and famous, so how could the Super consider it a dive? He also seemed to recall Dugs mentioning it by name when he told the Sergeant's staff meeting that they could moonlight to alleviate the overtime restrictions imposed because of a budget overspend, so long as it was in a reputable club like Roper's.

"Yes, sir. Sorry, sir."

"Sorry won't cut it, Sergeant. Is the report accurate?" the Super asked.

"I don't know, sir; I haven't seen it." The Super either failed to notice the sarcasm of the remark, or decided to let it pass.

"In essence, Sergeant, it states that you attempted an off-duty arrest of a female celebrity for snorting a class A narcotic right off the table at which she was sitting. This happened while you were moonlighting as a bouncer in the aforementioned club." The Super tried to raise one eyebrow then, which he thought would give him a menacing aspect, but both eyebrows went up, which made it appear as if someone had inserted a beat copper's truncheon in a most unwelcome orifice.

"Yes, sir." The DS only just managed to hold back the laughter trying to erupt from his gut. He did not find the situation in any way funny, but the look on the Super's face brought him to the brink of hysteria. Thumper was sure that laughing at Dugs in that moment would have been a negative career move.

"Since when, Sergeant, are you seconded to the narcotics division?"

"I am not, sir; I am with SO14."

"Yes, Specialist Operations Fourteen. Royal family and visiting dignitary protection," the Super mused. "And how do you think HRH would react to one of his personal protection detail getting their arses kicked by a celebrity bodyguard while moonlighting in a dive like Roper's?"

Thumper remained silent. He knew himself to be slightly challenged when it came to IQs, but despite that lack, knew when the question levelled at him had been rhetorical. The Super did not want a response, he just wanted to let off some steam and continue the downward flow of the shit storm that probably began with the Home Secretary and passed the Assistant Commissioner Specialist Operations en route to him, growing exponentially as it flowed. Despite his diminutive IQ, Thumper knew himself to be a good security officer. He was always first during competitions on the firing range, and always had a good eye for a threat. That Moses geezer getting one over on him in the club had been an aberration, just because his eyes were on the woman. When he saw her blatantly snort a line of coke from the table where she was sitting with several men, he had reacted with impulse, taken her head into an armlock and told her she was under arrest. He knew his sons drooled over her each time she appeared on Top of the Pops. Watching her snort a line so openly in a popular night spot caused something to break. She was a role model for the younger generations, for Christ's sake. How dare she set such a bad example?

At the time, he had not considered the possibility that one of the men might be a bodyguard. When he felt a kick to the back of his knee and his left leg crumple under him with an audible snap and an unbelievable pain, he realized his error. His immediate reaction was one of fury, but when he looked up from his half-crouch and saw the eyes of the man who had assaulted him, his fury vanished to be replaced by fear. He tried to tell himself it was wariness in the face of the unknown, but deep down he knew it was fear. The eyes were empty, showing nothing; no remorse, no fear, no anger, nothing. The woman had scrambled back from his grasp and he could see that she too was looking at his assailant, and that she too was afraid of him.

"Do you know who I am?" Thumper had asked.

As he thought about it now, standing with his balls in his hand in the Super's office, he realized how daft it sounded. How could the man possibly have known? Instead of answering the question, the assailant had shrugged his shoulders and crossed his arms, smirking at the idiocy of it. Other off-duty coppers were arriving at the scene by that time and Thumper had the decency to blush. He knew that three of the bouncers in the nightclub came from SO14 and that his embarrassment would be all over the men's changing room first thing in the morning. It would then be all over the Specialist Operations division shortly thereafter. He also knew that the Home Secretary was a friend of Roger Roper, the proprietor, so the shit storm he was now facing had been inevitable.

"Plod is on the way, Bunny," one of his colleagues told him. Thumper looked up and saw the eyes of his assailant twinkle with mirth at the nickname. He hated it, but in the SO you took what name you were given with good grace.

He dragged his mind back to the Super and said, "I'm sorry, sir. I missed that. Can you repeat?"

"Are you telling me, Thumper that you are not even listening? You are the width of a bollock hair away from getting the boot and you can't be bothered to listen to me?"

"No, sir. I mean yes, sir. I was distracted by the pain in my leg, sir."

The Super did not look convinced, but continued his carpeting. "I said the ACSO is considering disciplinary action against you for moonlighting." Dugs hesitated to allow the information to sink in. According to his file, DS Thumper needed slightly more time than the average man to grasp meanings. "There is a meeting of senior officers next week to discuss the implications and reach a decision on how to proceed. You can consider yourself on suspension from this moment until that decision is made."

"Suspended, sir? But why, sir? Is anyone else being suspended, sir?"

"No one else was caught with their trousers around their ankles and their cock in their hand, Sergeant." The DS knew his trousers were still around his ankles, only now he did not have his cock in his hand, but his arse in the air. He accepted the inevitability of that truth before something more important crossed his mind, "Will I be on full pay, sir?"

The Super let the question hang for a moment before responding. He felt he was entitled to at least a little fun after the Sergeant had ballsed-up so emphatically. However, looking at the hurt and seeing the calculation in the Sergeant's obvious thinking, calculation about how he might revert to the PCS, Public and Commercial Services Union, he conceded. "Yes, suspended on full pay."

The DS visibly relaxed at the news. Layla would not be pleased if their secondary source of income was also cut-off. Their primary source of income, his bouncing in the club, was definitely cut-off: with the displeasure of the Super and his broken knee, Thumper knew he would be out of action for quite some time.

"That is at least the official version," Dugs continued. "Unofficially, you will attach yourself to that Moses character and unleash the seven plagues upon him."

Thumper's lack of understanding was evident in the cut of his jaw. The Super sighed. "When we release him later today, you will attach yourself to him and cause his life to be a veritable hell until he slips up and we can throw the book at him."

"Release him, sir? Aren't we going to charge him with assault?"

"How can we charge him with anything, Sergeant, let alone assault? Charging him will make the whole thing public. We will have enough difficulty keeping it from HRH as it is, without publicising your fuck-up any further. So far, the gutter press has not latched on, and you should pray twice daily that that situation remains, because if it becomes public knowledge that one of SO14's personal security officers had the shit kicked out of them by a mere celebrity bodyguard, your feet will not touch the ground on your way out of The Yard."

Chapter 2

Inspector Izzo, Senior Investigator of Organized Crime in the region of Naples had a problem.

While Thumper was standing with his balls in his hand, Izzo was kneeling over a couple of corpses smoking a Gauloise, as he invariably did when investigating a murder. It helped to dull the smell that pervaded any murder scene. This killing appeared to be a particularly gruesome double execution. The men had been left in the foyer of the Juvenile Detention Centre on Via Nisida, not far from the entrance to the naval base just the other side of the bridge onto the island.

They had been shot in the back of the head at point blank range. Their sightless eyes would have been staring up at the early morning sky if the weapon used to shoot them had not been a heavy calibre, perhaps a forty-five with hollow point rounds. As it was, where the eyes had been, there was nothing but gore.

Izzo looked around the open foyer with an eye trained to detail. Scene of Crime Officers had already packed up and left, so he knew his leaving fag ash all over the scene was no longer an issue. He was on his knees beside the corpses making his own assessment, before they would be hauled off to the morgue in Cardarelli hospital, up the hill near the airport. The remnants of two black plastic industrial grade bin liners were scattered about the foyer, indicating that the men had been shot elsewhere and their bodies wrapped and then unwrapped on delivery to the island.

"What's your first impression?" he asked Brigadiere Capo (Staff Sergeant) Cipolle, who leant against the foyer wall with his arms crossed.

"Just an everyday Camorra hit, boss." Izzo nodded his agreement. At least on first viewing, it looked like a straightforward Camorra hit, but he wondered about the significance of the Juvenile Detention Centre. Why had the bodies been dumped and unwrapped here, of all places?

"Tell Manazotte I want the calibre and type as soon as he has them." Cipolle nodded and walked away to make the call to the forensic scientist. Watching Cipolle's back, Izzo made a mental note to investigate a possible connection between the inmates of the centre and the victims. It had been a risk for the assailants to dump the bodies in this location, and Izzo wanted to know why they had deemed it an acceptable one.

He did not yet know who the victims were, but that situation would remedy itself quickly. After his years of service in the DIA, he could spot a Camorrista at a glance. They carried tattoos of rank and various battle scars that made them easily identifiable, and were invariably very young. The life expectancy of a Camorra soldier was not high. The life of violence they chose was not a forgiving one and few of the men who ended up there made it beyond thirty. Not that they all chose the life. Izzo knew that many of them were forcibly recruited into the families they fought and died for.

Izzo frowned. There were no CCTV facilities mounted on the outside of the Detention Centre, the current warden wanted to instil a sense of trust in the youths he hosted and felt mounting cameras everywhere would destroy any chance of that happening. To further frustrate the senior organized crime detective in the Naples region, no one who his team had questioned thus far had seen or heard anything during the night. He was frustrated but not surprised. The custodians in this sort of establishment tended to be those who had been booted out of one of the more challenging posts like Poggioreale, or like the warden, their heads were so far up from where their bodies resided, they had no grounding in the same reality as those at street level.

It always amazed Izzo that the authorities thought handling youths of the city would be easier than handling their adult counterparts. In his trade, Izzo encountered as many murderous juveniles as adults. It did not take adulthood to hold a gun or possess the will to use it. The Naples area saw almost as many young adolescent Camorriste as those in young adulthood.

"Cipolle," he called over his shoulder.

"Yes, boss," the Sergeant replied as he sauntered over.

"Go down to the Naval Base and ask the guards if their CCTV cameras work."

"Sure thing, boss, but you know as well as I do the chances of anything technical working in this shithole of a city are pretty remote."

"I know, Cipolle, but we have to at least try." Izzo knew that his Sergeant's reluctance to go down to the gate had more to do with who was there than the likelihood of the technology not functioning.

He stood up and wiped the dust from the knees of his slacks. The Gauloise was still in his right hand, almost spent. He stopped smoking the cigarette to concentrate on Cipolle's walk up to the gate guards. Izzo could see by the demeanour of his subordinate that he did not want to approach the guards and ask for favours. The Inspector did not blame him. The base was military and the guards Carabineers. The arrogance of the Carabineers was legendary and Izzo knew they would not offer any form of assistance to another department or service without first making them stand on their heads and then ask very politely if it was at all possible, please and pretty-please with bells and whistles on. It always made him laugh, because Cipolle himself came from the Carabineers, but seemed to have forgotten that.

Things had improved though, because before the advent of the DIA, they would have outright refused to offer any assistance to another department or service. As the murder and serious crime Inspector in the DIA (Direzione Investigativa Antimafia), Izzo knew how things with the Black Cats had improved over the years. There was still room for improvement, but best not to expect miracles.

The Inspector knew before his Sergeant got back that his attempt had been fruitless, because of the dejected way he scuffed his feet in the street dust as he returned. "Don't tell me, the CCTVs are out of service?"

"Don't know, boss. The Black Cat is a Lieutenant and he refused to speak to me because I'm only a Staff Sergeant."

"How did he know you're a Staff Sergeant?"

"He wouldn't speak to me at all until I showed him my ID."

Despite it being only ten o'clock in the morning, the Inspector knew instinctively it was going to be a long day. He shook his head and walked down towards the gate where the officer stood resting on the balls of his feet with his hands behind his back. As Izzo approached he recognized the Lieutenant as the same Carabineer who had been in the apartment in Lucrino when he began the investigation of the O'Brien murder a year or so before. He had seemed more than eager to help during the investigation into the brutal murder of the young Irish girl and Izzo hoped he would show the same eagerness now.

"Morning, Lieutenant," he smiled as he approached.

"Good morning, sir, how can I help you?"

"Can you tell me whether your CCTV cameras are working and whether they are on?"

"And you are?"

"Are you kidding me? You know who I am. We worked a murder scene together only a few months since." The Carabineer remained silent and emotionless with his hands behind his back. "I am Inspector Izzo of the DIA." Izzo fumed.

"Do you have ID, sir?"

"Of course I've got ID, Lieutenant. I'm a police officer." The two men looked at each other for long moments before Izzo realized the Lieutenant was much less likely to back down. It was not in a Carabineer's make-up to be second best in a standoff. "I suppose you want me to show it to you, despite the fact we worked together at a murder scene?"

The Carabineer said nothing, just waited. Eventually Izzo took his badge out from his inside jacket pocket and handed it over. The Black Cat stared at it for long moments, as though trying to detect a forgery. Izzo felt like laughing. Better laughing than crying, he supposed, or giving the guy cornutti (the horns), which would only result in more truculence and possibly even a reprimand from his superiors.

As he handed the badge back, the Carabineer asked, "How can I help you, sir?"

"That CCTV camera there above the gate. The one pointing in the direction of the Juvenile Detention Centre entrance, does it work?"

The officer looked where Izzo was indicating and then shrugged his shoulders. "I could not possibly tell you that, sir, without the express permission of the base Commandant."

"Why not?"

"It's classified."

"Whether your CCTV camera is working is classified?"

"Yes, sir." Izzo did laugh then. He could not believe the lengths to which this organization would go to be as unhelpful as possible towards their colleagues in another service. It was as though they were on opposing sides.

"Put me through to the Commandant, please."

"The Commandant is indisposed at this moment, sir. Perhaps I can help you in some other way?"

The Inspector turned away from the Black Cat, cupped his hands into a speaking trumpet and shouted, "Cipolle, here now please."

The Sergeant ran over. He had worked with Izzo for many years and knew when the boss was losing patience. He also knew that when that happened, it was best to do whatever was asked as quickly as possible.

"Handcuff this man, Sergeant, he is under arrest for obstructing a murder inquiry."

"You cannot do this. You do not have jurisdiction over a military base!" the Carabineer shouted as the Sergeant took his cuffs off the utility belt hidden under his light summer jacket and put the soldier's hands behind his back.

As the Sergeant restrained the officer, Izzo kept one eye on the guards standing by the barrier. The guards remained completely still, apparently not expecting such a move and unaware how to react. The Inspector was relieved. The situation could easily have turned nasty, because the young conscripts were armed with automatic rifles.

"You're not on a military base, Lieutenant. You are out here on the street with me. Do it, Sergeant. Put him in the back of my car and keep him company."

The Inspector turned his back on the gate, lit another cigarette and waited. He was not surprised at how quickly the camp Commandant appeared after the arrest. Izzo guessed he had been watching the exchange on a CCTV monitor somewhere in the camp. It had been unusual to find a Lieutenant on gate duty and Izzo surmised that the Commandant sent him out to keep an eye on how the investigation progressed and probably to obstruct in any way he could. Izzo wondered if it was in their standing orders to be as obstructionist as possible.

"By what right do you think you can arrest a Carabineer officer in the execution of his duty?" the Colonel stormed as he bustled up to where Izzo calmly smoked his cigarette.

"I'm an Inspector in the DIA, and if I think the officer in question is obstructing a murder inquiry while executing those duties, I've every right to arrest him."

"I shall report you to your superiors."

"By all means Commandant, you are within your rights to do so. I feel it only fair to warn you however, that my superiors have very little interest in how I run my day-to-day affairs. I suspect they will tell you to resolve the issue yourself."

The Colonel looked a little pensive before demanding, "What is it that you want?"

"I want to know whether that CCTV camera is working?"

"Of course it's working. Why else would it be there?" This is Naples, the Inspector thought. Most equipment in Naples, would originally have had some purpose, it would invariably have been long since forgotten because the kit in question no longer worked.

He smiled and nodded. "I need to have the film from last night."

"Why didn't you say so before? We could have avoided all this fuss."

Izzo nodded and smiled and knew he would be waiting forever before that tape was in his hands. Where the bodies had been dumped would cause the higher-ups some concern. If the US Navy boys heard about it, the Italian Navy would be a laughing stock because they had not reacted to two bodies being unwrapped on their doorstep like early Christmas presents.

Chapter 3

Archibald Moses had an entirely different problem.

Archie's problem had an air of money and arrogance wafting from it like a cheap department store eau de toilette. At more or less the same time that Izzo was battling the bureaucracy of military echelons outside the naval base on the island of Nisida, Archie was looking at his problem across the cheap wooden table in the interview room where they had brought him the night before. The trip from Roper's nightclub was in the back of a Paddy Wagon, so he had no real idea where he was. The drive had taken a little longer than he would expect, so he guessed he was probably in an interview room in The Yard. That surprised him, because the arresting officers should have taken him to the Covent Garden nick, Roper's being in the vicinity.

"Bald Archie?" the Pro Bono lawyer asked. Archie could afford private legal counsel, but failed to see the benefit in spending a fortune when the judiciary provided the service for nothing. If his years in the orphanage had taught him anything, other than how to defend himself, it was frugality.

"A nickname the kids in the orphanage gimme on account o' me nob. It stuck when I was in The Sweeps."

Alliss nodded his acceptance of the explanation, even though he had not understood a word of it. Archie could read the misunderstanding in the lawyer's face, but rather than offer any clarification, he raised his eyes and looked at the mirror imbedded in the wall behind. He could see the neatly coiffured grey hair on the back of the man's head, which matched the neatly manicured nails and general air of money emanating from him. He had no doubt that if it had not been early on a Saturday morning, the lawyer would have been wearing a tailor-made Saville Row suit and not jeans and a tee-shirt. Archie knew instinctively that the man was a pillar of the community, a pillar that is, who represented everything Archie hated. In fairness, it was his own fault, but he had not expected to get this type of lawyer when he opted for Pro Bono counselling.

The interview room was compact, no more than eight feet by ten, and had no natural light, just a long neon bulb above the table, which had been buzzing since Archie was shackled to the chair. He loosened his bow tie and undid the collar stud of his dress shirt. It was unlike him to let his dress code slip, even slightly, but he had been sitting in this room all night and was beginning to feel the strain. At first his vigil was accompanied by a gaggle of detectives as they interviewed him, berated him, told him that they were going to send him down for life because of what he had done to one of their own. Archie refused to speak except for constantly demanding a lawyer. The more he demanded, the more frustrated the detectives became. Eventually there was only one left, a DS Standing, who demanded responses to his never-ending questions. As with his predecessors, each question was met with the same response.

"Please can I have a lawyer present."

That ordeal had seemed to last forever, but as he loosened his collar, Archie guessed it was still quite early on Saturday morning. Feeling slightly more comfortable, he continued to look at the man across the table, who was reading a report on the desk between them and throwing him occasional glances over the half-moon specs perched on the end of his nose.

The specs and their location gave the lawyer an air of arrogance that caused Archie's hackles to rise. Together with that arrogance the man oozed a sense of authority. Archie hated authority. Ever since he had been side-lined by the same crowd who had been the first to show him any respect. Side-lined because of a small defect over which he had no control. It was not his fault that he hated heights, or more specifically, flying at height with the open maw of a Hercules only feet away from where he was standing. Bastards did for him because he would not run out of the back of an airplane at twenty thousand feet. More fool them. He would have made a great soldier, as his ten years' celebrity bodyguarding had shown. He was a natural when it came to security. There was no one better. Celebrities now paid top dollar for his services when they visited England, Scotland, or Wales.

Philip Alliss looked at his charge and thought that it was hard to believe Archibald Moses was only thirty years of age. The obviously guilty man looked like he was at least in his forties. He raised a mental note to remove himself from the Pro Bono list. He was tired of defending the indefensible. The criminal sitting opposite him had one hand shackled to his chair because the police were uncomfortable with the idea of releasing him. Moses was a prime example of what made a Pro Bono defence lawyer's job so thankless. Besides, he had more important things to be doing than working with this violent man. He had forgotten he was on the duty roster when the phone rang the previous night. He had not been asleep at the time, but was sitting in his kitchen staring at the postcard from Naples, which arrived earlier that same day.

He looked at the man he was supposed to defend. Alliss guessed that when he referred to his nob, he meant his head and not any other anatomical part with which the noun might be associated. Philip flipped another page in the report. He was surprised at the speed with which The Met had obtained the military records of his charge, but guessed being in SO14 meant access to all sorts of fast track procedures. The team that were responsible for the protection of the Royal Family would doubtless be treated with some sort of priority when it came to cooperation between organizations. Alliss flipped to the cover of the report and saw that it was a Royal Military Police folder. He knew that the military police forces had a good working relationship with The Met, which would have helped to speed things along, no doubt.

"You served in the Royal Green Jackets for a time." Okay, that's what he meant by The Sweeps, Alliss guessed.

"Yeah, until they booted me out."

"There is no reason given on the file. Why were you discharged?"

"I don't see that's any o' your concern."

"I am attempting to get a feel for your character."

Archie snorted. "Why, what difference'll that make?"

"If we can demonstrate good character and a remorse for your actions in assaulting the police officer, the Crown Prosecution Service are less likely to push for a prosecution."

"I don't feel any remorse."

"You don't feel that striking a police officer is not the right thing to do?" Alliss was getting a feel for the man he was supposed to defend. He was glad in a way that no real defence would be required.

"I didn't know 'ee was a copper. 'Ee just grabbed me client 'round the neck and said 'ee was gonna do 'er."

"I find that hard to believe, Mr Moses. The officer in question said he told your client that she was under arrest."

Archie laughed, "I don't give a shit wotcha believe. Ee took 'er in a choke 'old and practically screamed I'm gonna do you, bitch."

The barrister made a note on his legal pad and flipped another page of Archie's record. "You are sure he did not mention that he is a police officer?" he asked as he continued to read.

"Course I'm fuckin' sure. Said ee' was gonna do 'er an' that was that."

"So, you acted in your client's defence?" Alliss had been a lawyer for many years and it never failed to amaze him how those caught in the act of whatever crime it was they had perpetrated felt that their lies were truly convincing when trying to excuse their actions.

"Right. Where I come from, when a bloke says they're gonna do a girl, it means only one thing."

"Yes quite, I see your point."

Alliss let it drop. It was the word of the SO14 officer against that of his client. There were seemingly no witnesses to what happened immediately before the assault. Despite being told to remain available for a statement, the pop star flew out of the country in her Learjet not long after the fracas in the nightclub, cancelling her tour of Britain with the excuse of laryngitis. None of the other celebrities in the club or colleagues of the police officer had been close enough to hear what the officer said to the woman, despite Archie's claim that he was screaming. It did not matter anyway. SO14 would not press charges. The Met division with the remit to protect the Royal Family could not afford the scandal of an expert officer being implicated in a club brawl while illegally moonlighting. Never mind that he had lost the brawl and suffered a broken knee in the process. No, they had already informed Alliss that they would not press charges. He guessed that they would cover up the incident and hope the 'Gutter Press' did not get hold of the story.

Alliss considered himself to be quite a good judge of character. He could see the malice in the eyes of his charge. There was no love lost between this person and any representatives of authority, that much was obvious. The lawyer stood, knocked on the door of the interview room and asked the guard to bring two coffees. "How do you take your coffee?"

Despite his instincts warning him not to trust this man, Archie was glad to be offered coffee. He was feeling the tiredness of not sleeping all night, and knew he needed to be alert, "Black, no sugar."

"You really must try to trust me," Alliss said placatingly when he handed the black coffee in a Met mug across the table. Moses just scowled at the mirror and shrugged his shoulders.

"When the police officer presses charges for assault against you, I will be your only friend."

"If 'ee presses charges, it'll be my word against 'is." Despite the statement, Archie knew he was in trouble. He knew in normal circumstances the word of one against another would not convince the Crown Prosecution Service to prosecute, but when one of them was a distinguished police officer, that all changed.

"Not so," Alliss seemed to perk up, as if he had just remembered something of importance. "We have a sworn statement from your client. A solicitor arrived at the Covent Garden police station with a signed statement from her at eight o'clock this morning." Archie grinned and nodded. It was now no longer his word against that of the establishment.

"It was delivered here at the same time I arrived." Archie watched the man shuffle through a pile of papers and select one.

"Here it is. I have not read it yet," he elaborated. Archie sat in silence while he did so, watching his facial expressions. The lawyer seemed to run a full gamut of emotions before putting the statement down on the table with a frown.

"She seems to have sided with the police."

"What?" Archie could not believe what he had just heard.

"Let's see. Yes, basically she states that the police officer is a friend of hers and that they were having a friendly wrestle when you assaulted him."

Archie's jaw seemed to lose control as his mouth fell open in shock. What the hell did she think she was doing? How could the woman have decided to lie blatantly and abandon him to the machinations of The Met and this annoying lawyer. He looked at the man and felt like screaming. Had he not been shackled to the chair, he probably would have leapt over the table and taken the smarmy git by the throat.

"I can help you get out of this predicament," Alliss said after a few moments. "I am a member of the same gentleman's club as the Commissioner. I can have a word in his ear and get the whole thing dropped."

"Why would you do that?" Archie asked, sure that there would be something required in return.

"I need a favour," so there it was out in the open.

"What sort of favour?"

"I need a missing person located."

"I'm a fuckin' bodyguard, nor a copper, nor a private investigator. Go to your local cop shop and report them missing, or get out the Yellow Pages 'n look for a PI."

"I have reported my son missing already, Mr Moses, but he is an adult, and the police have enough to be dealing with, without looking for someone who might not even be missing."

"What d'ya expect me to do?"

"With your background, I suspect you are not without a certain skill set."

Alliss did not want to iterate, but he suspected any search for his wayward son might result in a certain amount of heavy stuff. The boy was mixing with the wrong crowd to get back at Philip. Christopher had never forgiven his father for the death of his mother. Not that it was Philip's fault, but he had not been there during the crisis. The boy watched it happen and blamed his father.

"Christopher, Chris, is my son, and it is a delicate matter. A matter which needs to be handled with some discretion."

"Delicate how?"

"The boy never forgave me for the death of his mother." Archie did not understand how that amounted to a delicate matter, but let it drop. He knew he would probably have to submit to this man's demands if he was to guarantee that the CPS did not prosecute him for assaulting a police officer, however unbelievable the situation might be deemed.

"Where was 'ee when you last 'eard from 'im?"

Archie had no idea if that was the right question with which to start a missing person's investigation, but he had read enough Raymond Chandler to think that it might sound at least semi-professional. Besides, he had no idea how to begin, so he might as well start with the last known location. Anyway, he felt he could do with a bit of a trip after the events of the last several hours.

"He sent me a letter on stationary from a resto-pub in Gloucester, called The Pukka Duck." How apt, Archie thought. "I also have a photograph of him from just before he left home. They are still in my case from when I reported him missing."

The lawyer opened his briefcase and proffered the mentioned articles. "You will do it, then?"

"It seems like I don't have much choice, do I?"

Alliss shook his head in what he hoped was a conciliatory manner. All he needed was for Moses to call his bluff and his ruse would be over before it had even begun.

"Okay, if I get out of 'ere today, I'll go to Gloucester in the morning. I ain't gonna make any promises, though."

"I would only expect you to do the best you can, Archie." The lawyer used his first name, which he noticed but let slip. He had more important things to think about now he had accepted a job for which he had no qualifications.

"My bodyguard rates apply. Six 'undred a day, plus expenses."

"You won't regret it. I will get the release paperwork sorted out."

Chapter 4

Papa's problem was terminal.

Usually when faced with some sort of terminal illness, a person might tell their loved ones before confronting whatever treatment with a stalwart heart and a very British stiff upper lip, almost sure that the treatment would be ineffective. Not so for Papa. His cancer was sitting across the table from him in the shape of almost identical Latino men. Not twins or anything, he guessed, just so alike they could be mistaken for twins if seen at a distance. They wore the same Armani light summer suits, bespoke patent leather shoes, and Ray-Ban sunglasses.

Ray-Bans at four o'clock in the morning! Papa wondered which moron of the many he had encountered in his past life had sent these two clowns. He knew why they had broken into his Boston apartment in the early hours of a Saturday morning. It would not take a genius to work it out. Papa had been waiting for this moment for what seemed like all his adult life.

He looked across the table at the men. They seemed a little confused by his being in the kitchen when they broke in, like they expected him to be asleep. Papa did not sleep anymore though, not properly anyway. He grabbed a few minutes here and there during the day, so when they broke in, they found him sitting at his kitchen table drinking a glass of milk. He would have been drinking Cognac if he had had his way, but not withstanding the advice of his doctor, he could no longer stand alcohol of any description, never mind the hard stuff.

Anyway, Papa had been unable to sleep at night ever since he had played patty-cake with the secret service in the early eighties and shopped the Brigata Rossa. He felt no remorse at the time. They were the group who kidnapped and murdered a famous Christian Democrat, and Papa still felt that they deserved whatever they had coming to them. The Brigata Rossa did not take it kindly though. As soon as they realized his treachery, they went on the rampage and killed many of Papa's family and his closest associates. The death toll was into double figures before the secret service finally caught up with the killers and the slaughter stopped.

Even had he not breached every code that his clan lived by, Papa's life would have been forfeit. Those family members and associates who survived the massacre would never have forgiven him. He was forced to turn "pentito" or witness for the state and shop many of his Camorra peers. From that moment, Papa's life was owed in balance for the Brigata Rossa butcher's bill and those arrested because of his testimony. Although they had not been directly involved in the case, the FBI agreed to take him into witness protection in America as repayment for favours owed to the Italian Secret Service. Papa had been whisked away from

Poggioreale in an unmarked car with two burly Americans, given a new identity and settled in Boston as a baker.

He could bake. He had been a baker before getting a life sentence for murdering his sister's husband, because of a matter of honour. In all honesty, he would probably have been unable to keep faith had he been married to Bonfila, his sister, she was a dragon by anyone's standards. But that did not excuse the husband's crime. Being unfaithful was not the man's crime. Getting caught was the crime. Papa had loosed both barrels of his lupara into the man's face, while he sat on a milking stool in the street below their modest apartment in the Spanish Quarter. The crime would have gone unpunished except there was an American sailor in the street at the time. The sailor had a Kodak and he took a photograph of Papa as he walked away. Bad luck really, because the locals knew not to talk.

He did not mind too much, because shortly after arriving in Poggioreale he became a respected man. He had hated the imbalance of power that existed within the prison walls. He had seen Capi, or bosses, running the prison from within. Each had their own mini realm, as they had their own mini realm in Naples and its surrounds. When one of the Capi demanded that Papa pay homage to him, the baker became a man and killed him and his two guards with his bare hands. Piece by piece, he then built up his empire, which eclipsed any that preceded it. He became the most powerful man in Southern Italy. Those were the heady days before it all collapsed because the Red Brigade became too complacent about who they killed and Papa had been forced to break all the codes in which he firmly believed.

Since that fateful day, he had waited for this one to arrive. He knew it would come. It would only be a matter of time before someone who knew his "secret" location and new identity would find something more valuable that they needed and so would trade.

Papa smiled at the man who had a big silver gun levelled at his chest. He did not know guns, so had no idea what it was. When he was sent to Poggioreale in the nineteen-sixties, he had used a lupara not a big swanky American gun like this man held. He had been a baker, not a Camorrista.

"The secret service gave you up," the man with the gun said.

Papa shrugged. He had always known it would be the secret service. They were the weak link in the chain if for no other reason than their complete lack of loyalty. As soon as they required something from the family, they would give up his location for that service, whatever it might be. He knew that. He was just surprised at how long it had taken. It was nineteen-eighty-one when he rolled over from his position of power in Poggioreale prison. It was now nineteen-ninety-seven. Not many diagnosed with cancer lasted for sixteen years.

The other one, the one without a gun said, "Say cheese," as he snapped a photo. The flash blinded Papa momentarily and when he regained his sight the camera had vanished as quickly as it had appeared.

"So, what are you going to do to me," Papa asked? He knew the answer, of course. He was just playing the game. One of the old associates wanted him dead, but he guessed the morons sitting opposite had instructions to make his suffering last.

The man who did not have a gun trained on him stood and walked over to Papa's chair. He picked up a tea-towel from the towel rack as he came. Papa smiled at the man as he approached, until the tea-towel was forced into his mouth, which assumed a rictus that prevented him from smiling any further.

"I am going to enjoy this," the man said with a smile, as he started to strip Papa of his nightclothes.

By the middle of the afternoon after his bout on the Super's carpet, Thumper was sitting in his wife's pink Fiat 500 automatic feeling like an arse. He was very tired. The ambulance that came to Roper's during the night took him to Saint Pancras hospital Accident and Emergency. It was after four o'clock in the morning when he was discharged, encumbered with a Plaster of Paris cast, a plastic beaker of powerful painkillers and a nagging wife.

The trip home had been excruciating, not only because of his leg, but also because Layla bleated in his ear from the hospital car park to their ramshackle apartment in Peckham; by the time they were in the lift to the third floor, Dick Thumper was sick of hearing about how she hated to "miss a full eight hours, especially just before a tournament weekend". With the noise echoing between his ears he went to bed and dropped off instantly, only to get two hours of fitful sleep before his office mobile rang.

"Dugs needs you in his office, Sergeant." The Super's PA did not waste time with small talk.

"What time," he slurred?

"Preferably the day before yesterday."

It had been just after eight o'clock in the morning when he stumped into the Super's office like a disgruntled Ahab on steroids. The interview had been the worst forty-five minutes of his career, and was why he now sat cramped, in pain and dishevelled, in an area of the city where he seldom came.

Thumper kept playing the grilling over in his mind. Basically, the Super instructed him to attach himself to Moses and build a case against him. The DS had no idea how he would manage to do that. He felt that Moses was not a criminal, an arsehole maybe, but not a criminal. Finding evidence against him would be hard, if not impossible. He knew that his colleagues in other branches of The Met were not opposed to fitting up the occasional villain when it was the only way to get them banged up, but a man who was guilty of nothing more than defending his client? Thumper did not want to be party to that sort of activity, despite the constant throbbing in his leg being a reminder of what Moses did to him.

It was bad enough that he had to chase after a man who he considered to be more than likely innocent, or else lose his job, but to do so in a pink girlie car. He had wanted to put his foot down and tell Layla that he needed the Toyota, but knew it would mean months of misery to do so. Crossing Layla when it came to the bridge club was tantamount to high treason. His half-hearted attempt of, "But it's pink," did not sway his wife. Layla needed the Toyota for the weekend's club match in Brighton, so the DS would just have to make do with the Fiat. "I'm supposed to be on undercover surveillance."

"You should have thought about that before. I can't fit six bridge club members in the Fiat." Thumper had stomped out in frustration, his only option when it came to disagreements with Layla. He used the hall phone to ring the Super and try to get an unmarked car allocated.

When he asked if he could have a car for the assignment, the Super just laughed. "What did I tell you in the meeting this morning, Sergeant?"

Thumper thought back. The Super had been adamant that the operation was to be completely under the radar, so an unmarked car was a non-starter. Then Dugs told him that he would have to pay for the operation and was to consider it punishment for allowing Moses to get one over on him, which did nothing to improve the Sergeant's mood.

He frowned at the steering wheel. He was a big bloke and sitting in a bubble car was an uncomfortable experience, made even more so because his left leg was in a plaster cast and stuck out before him. He had been parked in Cromwell Road behind a tree for a little over an hour and his buttocks already ached even more than his knee, despite him spending two hours in the gym every day. He was not a fitness freak or anything. It was as much to get away from Layla as to keep himself in shape, a habit that would remain until he finally plucked up the courage to ask for a divorce. He laughed at himself. His plucking up the courage to ask for a divorce was about as likely as the Super calling off the 'witch hunt' on Moses. He got out of the car to smoke a cigarette. Layla had rules about smoking in their cars. He could smoke in a police car as much as he cared to, but not in the Fiat or the Toyota.

The DS lit up and frowned. He knew he was in for the long haul. Following Moses to Cromwell Road after his release from The Yard was just the beginning. He had watched the man enter a Georgian townhouse, which was no doubt converted into apartments. Thumper supposed most inner city properties had been converted and what looked from the front like a posh terraced house with Roman columns, would have country mansion prices attached to it. He had briefly glanced at the report on Moses, and so knew that he came from an underprivileged background, but the DS still begrudged the wealth the bodyguard seemed to enjoy.

Archie pulled the net curtains back very slightly and looked at the police officer hiding behind a tree beside the pink car he had used to follow the taxi. Archie spotted the tail when he was flagging down the taxi out the front of The Yard. From the bulk behind the wheel and the close cropped blond hair, he guessed it was the same copper he had smacked in the club the night before. It was like something out of a Blake Edwards film. Who would conduct a stakeout in a pink car? It was ludicrous. As the thought crossed his mind, a plume of smoke emerged from behind the tree. Archie stifled a laugh. Not only was the copper conducting a stakeout in a pink car that was far too small for him, he was smoking behind a tree while trying to be inconspicuous.

He cast his mind back to the meeting in the interview room. It felt like the lawyer had winded him with a sledge hammer when he said, "She seems to have sided with the police officer."

The more Archie thought about it, the more confused he became. Why would she lie like that? He guessed she would have been worried about repercussions because of the class A drug, but why lie? She could just have said nothing. He was not only confused, but angry. He had served her well each time she came to London, so why deny the events of the night and side with the copper?

Archie knew he needed to let it drop, because he had a more pressing issue to consider. He needed to think about how he would deal with the lawyer's request. He did not take too well to being blackmailed, but he had little choice. He knew that Alliss had him over a barrel and obviously intended to get as much out of the situation as he could. He doubted that the CPS would prosecute him when none of the three witness statements agreed, but it was feasible that as soon as the woman's statement became common knowledge, the officer would be encouraged to change his to coincide with hers so they could press charges. That is what

Archie would have done in a similar situation. Although each of the relevant parties already had copies of his original statement, Archie knew the copper could cite the stress of pain caused by a broken knee as the reason why he had misremembered. Archie was sure that false testimony from Met officers had happened before and would happen again. It was the nature of the territory. It was the reason why Archie had agreed to find the lawyer's son.

He was not sure that he believed the story that the lawyer told him in the interview room. It was probable that the son was missing, but he was sure something else was going on. Alliss might want him to find the boy, but not because he was worried about him. He could tell by the man's nervous disposition that there was something of much greater importance happening. The mood swing in the interview room that morning had been immediate. Archie had watched the range of facial expressions that crossed Alliss's face as he read the statement. He saw it light up when he realized that some sort of an opportunity had presented itself.

He took the photograph of Christopher Alliss and the letter out of his inside jacket pocket. He had glanced at the letter briefly in the taxi and it had seemed a little odd. It was not the letter of a loving son who a father would worry about when missing. "Feeling a longing for the old country. Chris."

That was it, brief and to the point. It did not mean much to Archie. He supposed it meant more to the lawyer, but it was obvious that he would not be forthcoming with any information he deemed unnecessary to locate his son. And where was the old country anyway? Gloucester? It did not seem likely. Archie also wondered why the lawyer had handed the letter over. He could just have easily told him the name of the pub.

He let the curtain drop back into place and moved over to the drinks cabinet. He would drive down to Gloucester in the morning and see where the day led from there. He hoped that on arriving in the West Country city, he would find the boy in the resto-pub and discover that Alliss Senior's worries were nothing more than the usual pangs of parenthood, but he doubted it. Something did not feel right. He had agreed to a task that he somehow knew would take a long time fulfilling.

Archie decided to have a glass of whisky and then go to bed for an early night. It had been a long day, or more specifically a long night, and the next was not going to get any shorter. There was a drive down the M4 in the rush hour to face, never a good start to the day, never mind while being tailed by a fat copper with a broken leg in a little pink bubble car.

Chapter 5

The DS looked up from the previous day's paper just as Moses drove past in a black Maserati with gold trim. It was lucky he looked up when he did, otherwise he would have lost Moses before the operation had even begun. He had feared telling Layla that he had lost his secondary income, but telling her he had lost both would be suicide.

Thumper was even more tired than he had been the day before, because he had spent a sleepless and uncomfortable night in the Fiat 500, during which time he smoked forty cigarettes and quaffed half his painkillers. His fear of Layla's reaction if he stank out her car withered into dust during the night. The ashtray looked like an open crematorium urn and there was a pile of spent butts outside the car window, but only a few beside the tree. His only break came when he took what he considered to be a limited risk and drove to a twenty-four-hour Asian shop in a seedier area of the city at three o'clock in the morning, guessing that Moses would be asleep. He bought a paper, sixty cigarettes and two ready-made stale sandwiches from the half-asleep shop assistant and returned to Cromwell road to continue his stakeout. Two empty fag packets and the half-eaten sandwiches now littered the passenger seat as testimony to his vigil.

Thumper started the engine, but waited until Moses had gone some distance before pulling out into the early morning traffic. He tried to keep the Maserati in sight without getting too close. It was a near impossible task, because the sports car was low to the ground and almost completely hidden by traffic. It was too early for the normal rush-hour gridlock, so the DS just managed to keep tabs on the car. He followed as it changed lanes after the Cromwell Road became the A4. The Sergeant guessed they were heading for the M4 motorway. That realization made him a little nervous. He doubted if someone willing to assault a person in a nightclub would have any qualms about breaking the speed limit on a motorway. If he exceeded the limit, there would be no way for the Fiat to keep up. Thumper put it out of his mind and concentrated on keeping the car in sight. He would deal with issues on the motorway as they arose. If he had picked up anything during his years in the police, it was pragmatism.

Thumper was surprised how light the traffic was, before he remembered that it was holiday season and many of those who should be sitting in gridlocked rush-hour traffic were instead basking in the sun somewhere. He could easily see the Maserati about a hundred yards in front travelling in the fast lane. He knew that as they drove through the city he was not likely to encounter many problems. In London, the M4 was only two lanes. Issues were more likely to arise when they made it out into the countryside and the road widened into three lanes.

About thirty minutes after the chase commenced, Thumper was driving on auto-pilot. He had had no time to get a coffee and felt the tiredness weighing down on him. He bent down to tune the radio to a rock station in the hope it would keep him alert. When he looked up, the sports car was passing a long-haul vehicle, which immediately pulled into the middle lane to pass another truck. The DS pulled into the outside lane and willed the Fiat to a speed that meant he had at least a small chance of re-sighting Moses. But when he managed to pass the truck, there was no sign of the Maserati.

Thumper looked frantically in his rear-view mirror for any possible exits that he might have missed, but there were none. All he could see was the long-haul vehicle he had just passed and a couple of cars in the middle lane. There was no sign of an exit and no sign of his quarry. The DS started to thump the steering wheel in time with an elegant commentary on the situation: shit, shit, shits. He was considering pulling off the motorway at the next services exit when he glanced over his right shoulder and saw the Maserati beside him in the fast lane. How the fuck did he do that, Thumper thought?

For what seemed like an age, Moses stared at him grinning before he thumbed his nose and put his foot down. Thumper was already doing seventy and knew that the Fiat would shake its guts out if he tried to go any faster. He stared after the quickly vanishing sports car and decided that he would pull off at the next services and get a coffee as a sort of Dutch Courage before calling the Super and telling him it was off.

About an hour later, he was sitting in a services café nursing a cup of coffee. His mind had been in a whirl for thirty minutes or so before a possible solution came to him. He had resigned himself to calling the Super and admitting defeat when he glanced over at the tills where the motorway users paid for their petrol, and he saw a bank of active CCTV monitors. He knew people in the Traffic Division and some of them owed him favours. The motorway system in the UK was one of the most heavily infested CCTV zones in the world. The Maserati was far from inconspicuous. Someone must have seen it. He left the cold coffee on the table and walked over to the bank of public phones beside the toilets. He looked at them and regretted that he could not afford a personal mobile phone. He dialled his mate in traffic and told him the problem.

"I can't promise it will be quick, Dick," his colleague said.

"No problem, I will hang here 'til you call back."

In the end, it was only a few minutes later when the phone rang. He answered.

"Got some good news, Dick. The boys were watching the Maserati this morning. They have a sort of game where they keep tabs on a car, one each, like. Whoever keeps the car in sight for the longest gets the pot."

"Where, Dave, where?" The DS interrupted. He hung up a few moments later with his first smile since being kicked in the back of the knee in Roper's.

Archie felt a real sense of elation when he thumbed his nose at the daft copper in the pink Fiat and put his foot down. The car seemed to lift off the tarmac as the gears bit and he raced away. The Maserati was doing over one hundred miles per hour in a few seconds and the pink spec dwindled to nothing in no time at all. He eased off the pedal as soon as he was sure that the giant blond would not be able to catch him and began to think about how he would talk to the owner of the pub. As a civilian, he could not approach the man in an official capacity. The publican would not be obliged to help him. Archie knew his demeanour was not one that instilled confidence in people. They tended to be afraid and therefore wary of talking to him. He need not have worried, because the owner of the pub just referred him to the head chef who was more than willing to talk about Chris Alliss.

"Fuckin' charlatan, that's what that boy is."

Archie nodded in sympathy and encouragement. "How so?"

"Showed up here applying for a job as sous-chef. Had all the right references and qualifications. Seemed like a nice bloke, so I took him on."

"So how long did he work for you?"

"You must realize how busy we are here."

"Yes, of course. I heard you are the best resto-pub in Gloucester, of course you are busy."

"Yes, it was a couple of weeks before I realized that he was not what he claimed. I usually keep an eye on the new sous, but like I said, just too busy."

Archie raised his eyebrows and nodded his sympathy. "So, you noticed he was not up to scratch," he prompted.

"Yeah, food started to come back with complaints. Patrons who'd been here before and were used to a certain quality. So, I asked him to make me an omelette for lunch one day, as a test, like."

"And I am guessing it was not up to the required standard."

"The omelette was well formed, but he didn't season it." And Archie guessed not seasoning an omelette was a cardinal sin for a sous-chef.

"Do you have an address for him." The chef nodded and opened a filing cabinet from which he extracted a small white card. Armed with the address Archie thanked him and left.

Half an hour later he was standing on the doorstep of a terraced house in the outskirts of the city talking to a woman wearing curlers with a cigarette hanging from the corner of her mouth and the bloodshot eyes of someone who was never without one. "I don't suppose he left a forwarding address?"

"No, no time for that. I booted him out for not paying his rent. Threw his bags out the window. Followed 'em with his clothes. Wasn't feeling charitable enough to put the clothes in the bags."

Archie frowned. He was about to back down the stairs when the woman seemed to remember something. "He was dating a floozy, Ann something. She's a teacher, but works part time in the Cock 'n Bull in the city centre."

Thirty minutes later Archie ducked in through the back door of the pub, which was just off Northgate street, near the station. It was a little too dingy for Archie's taste. He preferred the sort of place that London city centre offered, like the Cromwell Arms near where he lived, which was light and airy with sawdust on the floor. Not because it was rough, but because the owner was trying to create an ambiance of the seventeenth century, to the extent that the bar girls' costumes exposed a huge amount of cleavage and they wore bob caps.

He walked up to the bar and enquired after Ann.

"I'm Ann," said the diminutive blond-haired barmaid nearest to him.

"Good day to you. I am looking for a young man called Christopher Alliss." The outwardly pleasant nature of the girl vanished immediately.

"What the hell do you want with that plonker?" she asked.

"Plonker? Why do you think he's a plonker?"

Ann noticed that the man had not answered her question. She eyed him warily, before deciding he was not as dangerous as he first appeared. Despite looking very hard and bald, he wore an expensive suit and spoke with a cultured London accent. She surmised that he was probably working for Chris's dad at the law firm.

"He left without saying goodbye."

Archie nodded in sympathy. "Bit of a rascal, then?"

"Yes, he is, I should never have allowed him into my bed." Archie smiled, as much to hide his embarrassment as anything. He was not used to girls talking about their sex lives so freely. In fact, he was not used to girls talking about sex, full stop. Archie's encounters with the other gender were usually paid for and fleeting.

"You didn't answer me. Why do you want him?"

"His father urgently needs to contact him." Archie kept the information to a minimum, not sure how much he should tell the girl. "Do you know where he is?"

"As far as I know, he is in Eindhoven in Holland."

"The Netherlands." The girl was not sure whether Archie was correcting her or asking for clarification.

"Yes, The Netherlands."

"How can you be sure?"

"He sent me a letter asking me to join him. He was getting a job as a sous-chef."

"And this upset you because?"

"It was the first I heard that he'd left."

"How do you know it was from Eindhoven? I mean he could have been lying."

"No, I saw the postmark on the envelope."

"And you are sure it was Eindhoven?"

Ann was getting annoyed. How many times could one person ask the same question before they believed the response. "I collect stamps, I still have the envelope upstairs in my apartment. I can run and get it for you if you like."

"That would be very kind. Thank you."

The girl was back within the space of a few moments and as promised had an envelope with an Eindhoven post mark. There was no letter though. "The letter?"

"I sent it back."

He felt a little awkward for having asked the same question repeatedly, and then prying into the whereabouts of the letter. He could tell the girl was getting annoyed by it all.

"Do you have anything more to go on, other than Eindhoven?"

"He said he was going to get a job in a restaurant called Le Pied de Cochon. I am a French teacher and I remembered the name because it seemed odd for a restaurant in a Dutch city to have such a similar name to a famous restaurant in Paris."

"So, he might have been making it up?"

"He might have been."

Archie thanked Ann and left. As he walked to his car, he frowned. A trip to Gloucester had seemed appealing. A trip to The Netherlands was less so. Not that he minded a drive to the Continent, but he had accepted the job from the lawyer in the expectation that a road trip to Gloucester would see it finished. For it to turn into an Odyssey had not been foreseen and was not welcome.

Thumper was about to give up and find a phone box to call the Super when he saw the Maserati parked in front of a pub called The Cock 'n Bull. He probably would not have noticed the car, but his long drive and crawling reconnaissance through the streets of Gloucester had caused him to develop a thirst. With a tongue that felt like it was coated with asbestos, he glanced down a side street, saw the Cock dancing in front of the Bull and drove the Fiat into the street. It was as he was pulling into the car park at the back of the pub that he saw the Maserati almost completely hidden in a shady spot under a lamppost a little down from the main entrance.

The DS whistled and felt an overriding sense of relief. If he had been forced to make a call to the Super admitting defeat, he knew his job would not have been there for him when he returned to the city. He was about to get out of the Fiat and go into the pub when Moses ducked out through the front door and made his way to the Maserati. Thumper considered briefly taking up the chase again before realizing it would be a waste of time. While there was such a discrepancy in the specifications of the vehicles they drove, giving chase would be an exercise in futility. No, he guessed that the way forward would be to act like a detective and do a bit of detecting.

He waited for Moses to leave and then went into the saloon bar, both for a drink and, hopefully, information on what his new nemesis was up to. The saloon bar was low-ceilinged and dark. The sort of place where shady characters congregate because their faces are in perpetual shade and no one could give a description to the police if one was ever required.

He wandered over to where the bar was located and ordered a pint of lager and a pork pie. Surprisingly, as there were very few customers, there were three bar staff. He thought he could tell which of the barmaids Moses had been talking to. There was only one with the same air of exasperation DS Standing had shown after he had interrogated Moses for several hours. Standing did not say much more than "I need a fuckin' drink", but that coupled with his expression, was enough for Thumper to realize how the interview had gone.

He paid and wandered over to the end of the bar where the girl was banging glasses into a dishwasher. "You wanna be careful you don't break one, could get a nasty cut."

"Who the fuck're you, Health and Safety?"

"Close," Thumper grinned as he showed her his warrant card. She frowned and assumed the resigned attitude that the DS was used to seeing after he flashed his warrant. "You got any mustard?"

"English, or French?"

"English. I find French anything a little too smooth for me." He grinned, willing her to share in his joke. She did not, but just frowned at him with crossed arms. "I'd say at a guess, you're pissed off cos you just had an encounter with Moses."

"So, you're a mind reader now?"

"Naw, not at all. I just recognize the symptoms. What's your name, sweetheart?"

"Ann. What happened to your leg?"

"Moses happened to my leg."

"Looks painful. You drive down from London like that?" Thumper nodded.

"How?"

"Car's automatic. Just rest me left leg on the footrest."

"I see. So, who's Moses anyway, apart from the parter of the Red Sea I mean?"

"Shortish Cockney, wide as a barn door and twice as thick."

"You mean that cultured type from the law firm with a posh London accent? He just left."

Thumper was confused then. He did not think anyone would describe Moses as cultured. He had not heard him speak, not even in the nightclub, but just assumed his accent would be from the gutter, the same as Thumper's. He frowned, but nodded his agreement.

"What was he after?"

"He's looking for my ex, Chris Alliss."

"What, Alliss like the lawyer?"

"Chris's father is a lawyer."

"Did he ever tell you his father's name?"

"No, just moaned a lot about him. Seems that he came out when Chris was still in the sixth form. Never forgave him." Thumper thought back then to what he knew about the lawyer. He remembered someone who was extremely suave and sophisticated, so could quite possibly be gay. He thought that the boy Moses was looking for was more than probably the lawyer's son.

"Did he say what he wanted with him?"

"No, just that his father was urgently trying to contact him."

"That's strange," the DS mused, wondering what possible motive Moses could have for seeking out the lawyer's son. Was he looking for some sort of revenge, or leverage maybe? What? He quite visibly relaxed though, because he knew instinctively that he might just have been given the means he would need to satisfy the Super's wishes. There was no way that Moses going after the boy was legitimate. The chances that he could catch Moses up to no good now seemed greatly improved.

"What did you tell him?"

"I showed him an envelope I got from Eindhoven."

"From the Alliss boy?" She nodded.

Thumper took another slug of lager as he tried to digest the information. He guessed that his quarry would now be heading for Eindhoven.

"Do you think he is going there?" he asked the girl for confirmation.

"Yeah, I reckon so. He seemed resigned to the fact that he would need to go."

Thumper thought some more. He could not go to the continent without first getting permission from the Super. Normally, travelling chits were signed by the Detective Chief Inspector, but the Super had been very clear about what the reporting chain would be for this operation. The DS was to contact no one other than the Super, not under any circumstances.

"Great, thanks, Ann." Thumper quaffed his lager in one pull and was leaving his bar stool with pork pie in hand to go and make a call to the Super when the girl stopped him.

"Wait." She said before running out of the bar. She returned a few minutes later waving a postcard. "The reason I was banging the glasses is I was angry at myself. I received a postcard after the letter, from a place called Pozzuoli. I completely forgot about it."

A few minutes later the DS was on the phone to Dugs. "You are sure he does not know of the move?"

"No, sir. I mean yes, sir. He's gone to a place called Eindhoven, wherever the hell that is."

"Are you eating, Sergeant?"

Thumper cursed and swallowed a lump of unchewed pie, "No, sir, just a bad line, sir."

"It is in the Netherlands, Sergeant."

"The Netherlands?" He thought the netherlands was a polite way of referring to his balls.

"Holland, Sergeant, Holland. And you say the Alliss boy is now in somewhere called Pozzuoli?"

"Yes sir."

"My guess is that Moses will eventually arrive in Pozzuoli, and that we have an opportunity to get ahead of him." The Super seemed to be thinking aloud rather than asking Thumper for an opinion. "Why is he after the Alliss boy?"

"I don't know, sir. My only guess is that it can't be for anything legit. Leverage maybe? Revenge?"

"Revenge for what, Sergeant? The lawyer got him off, or at least that's what the lawyer would have told him, I'm guessing. But whatever it is, it's sure to be illegal, Sergeant."

"Yes, sir. I think so, too. Do you think I should go to this place called Pozzuoli, sir?"

"Yes, Sergeant."

"I cannot afford a trip to Italy, sir."

"No, of course not. You keep all your receipts and I will pay using the slush fund."

"Thanks sir."

Thumper was about to hang up when the Super spoke again. "Well done Dick, you've been on the job for what, twenty-four hours, and already you are going places. Well done."

"Thanks, sir."

"By the way, where is this Pozzuoli?"

"The postmark says Italia, sir, which I guess is Italy."

"Okay, Sergeant, I will get one of the lads to look it up. You call me back here in one hour and I will tell you how to proceed."

Four hours later that Sunday evening, DS Thumper was in his Peckham apartment sawing at his plaster cast with a bread knife. He had a long drive in front of him and the discomfort of a plaster cast was not an option. He had stopped off in the local pharmacy en route and bought one of those knee support things favoured by athletes. The pharmacist had been sceptical about refilling his subscription, but had relented when the DS showed him his warrant card and said he was going away on duty for at least a week. With his leg strapped up and the pain dulled with the imitation opiates he climbed once more into the pink Fiat and set off for the south of Italy. Layla had not been back from bridge, so he left her a note on the kitchen table. He was glad, because had she been there, he knew he would still be in the kitchen arguing the toss.

Chapter 6

Early the next morning, Superintendent Douglas sat looking at the telephone on his desk for long moments before finally conceding and picking it up. Escalating to the Chief was not something that Dugs would do on a whim. The Chief did not like escalation and especially escalation that would not stop at his desk. He believed that the natural world order should not be challenged and that shit should only travel downwards before eventually coming to rest on the shoulders of a junior police constable, preferably one who had only been in the service for five minutes. Dugs knew that approaching the Chief Super could be a career-threatening move. He liked his career and was not exactly happy about putting it in the sights of any punishment-serving superior officer. But what could he do? Progressing without the approval of his immediate superior *would* be the end of his career, no threat required. It had to be done. Finally accepting the inevitability of it, he dialled the three-digit extension for the Chief Super's office. The phone was answered on the first ring by the Chief's assistant.

"Hi Peggy, it's Superintendent Douglas. Can I speak to the Chief?" He waited while Peggy connected him, looking at the portrait of the Queen behind his desk and holding his breath.

Chief Superintendent Rogers-Smythe sat staring at the portrait of the Queen behind his desk after he ended the telephone conversation with Superintendent Douglas. He knew that he needed to call the Commander, but the Commander hated escalation even more than Rogers-Smythe. Careers had been ended on less, and Rogers-Smythe was one of the youngest Chief Supers in the history of The Met. That flying rise was likely to come crashing down in Icarus style, all because some Detective Sergeant had taken it upon himself to get clobbered in Roper's night club by little more than a paid wet-nurse. And not only did he get clobbered in spectacular fashion, it was also in front of three of his peers from SO14 and half the celebrity world. Why could he not have acted the hero in some local fish and chip shop where no one would have seen, or cared? Unfortunately, Rogers-Smythe knew that he did not have the authority to do what needed to be done and would no more go above the head of the Commander than he would spit on the portrait behind his desk, so he steeled himself and made the call.

"Hi Sue, it's Chief Superintendent Rogers-Smythe. Can I speak to the Commander?"

Commander Willett did not have a portrait of the Queen behind his desk, because when one reached the rank of Commander, sucking up to Her Majesty was no longer included in the job description. He replaced his portrait with a nice print of a

Constable landscape. The Commander loved Constable's work, because it reminded him where he began life in The Met, not as a ranker, of course, but out in the countryside at the Police Academy in Hendon. He was as nervous as the others had been about calling his superior. The Assistant Commissioner was a known stickler for etiquette and did not want to be bothered with the day-to-day running of the division for which he was responsible. He would find the need to be involved in daily police affairs to be at the very least unsavoury, but more probably as something that would require the meting out of summary justice, and Willett knew where summary justice normally landed. However, he also knew that he could do nothing without the Assistant Commissioner, and so picked up his phone and dialled the extension for the ACSO's PA.

"Morning, Margery, Commander Willett. Can I speak with the Assistant Commissioner?"

The Assistant Commissioner frowned at the portrait of the Queen behind his desk as he listened to Willett's request. He liked having a portrait of the Queen behind his desk, because it reminded him to whom he owed his allegiance and duty. The more he listened to Willett, the more he wished he was duty bound to the first Queen of the name, at least then he could have beheaded his wayward subordinates.

"Let me see if I understand you? Superintendent Douglas set his dog onto the character who incapacitated him in that inner-city nightclub the other night?"

"Yes, sir."

"And now his dog is following a lead and Superintendent Douglas has sent him to some place called Pozzuoli near Naples?"

"Yes, sir."

"And you want me to do what, exactly?"

"We think our counterparts in the Italian police might get a little jumpy about an SO14 operative showing up in their backyard with a gun."

"What do you mean, with a gun?"

"He is an armed protection officer, sir. He has a gun."

"I thought he was suspended?"

"Officially sir, that is the case. Unofficially, he is investigating the Moses case."

"What Moses case, Commander?"

The ACSO's frown was becoming more pronounced as the discussion went on. It always amazed Assistant Commissioner Bond how inept officers managed to gain such senior ranks. These men were his highest executives, not too far removed from the position the Queen herself held. There was no excuse for not doing as they had been told. They were supposed to brush the whole affair under the proverbial rug and hope it went away, not start a witch hunt for some celebrity bodyguard, who, by the way, was guilty of nothing more than protecting his client. The telephone call lasted for several more minutes before the AC replaced the receiver and stared at it trying to think who best to call to sort out the mess that his subordinates had created. One thing he knew for sure, after the day's fiasco had been resolved, heads would roll, despite Her Majesty being the second of her name.

Inspector Izzo was bending paperclips into animal shapes while sitting behind his rickety desk in the station in Pozzuoli when the phone rang. He was finding doing a swan particularly difficult, partly because he had never seen a swan except on the television, but mostly because the paperclips had decided to act the maggot and not bend to his will. Whenever he had something on his mind he resorted to playing with paperclips and smoking too many cigarettes. He stared at the phone, resenting the interruption, angry at himself for forgetting to turn the telephone off, but his conscience would not allow him to ignore it once it had started to ring, so he picked it up.

"Pronto," he barked.

"Inspector Izzo?" The inspector held the receiver away from his face and frowned for a few seconds. It was very unusual for him to hear his name mispronounced in English on the telephone in the Pozzuoli office. In fact, he could not remember ever having received a phone call in English on any telephone.

He put the phone back to his ear and said, "No, it is pronounced I T S O. Not I Z Z O."

"Yes, quite," the Englishman conceded. "You are the inspector responsible for investigating organized crime in the Naples region?"

The Inspector did not answer immediately. His mind was elsewhere. As he knew it would, the CCTV footage from the naval base at Nisida had taken an age to arrive. He and Cipolle had studied it earlier that morning and it proved to be not worth the wait. The footage showed a van pulling up at the foyer of the Juvenile Detention Centre and two men dumping the bodies. One of the men kept his face hidden from the camera, as if he knew where it was, and the other, despite lacking his compatriot's shyness, was an unknown. It was the stark contrast between the two men that was causing Izzo to worry his paperclip supply into little ducks and ponies, but not swans. How could two Mafiosi out on a job together display such a stark contrast in their abilities? The conclusion was not one that he wanted to accept, because it made his line of inquiry much more difficult to follow. If one of the men was not a Mafioso, that meant he was an outsider and for an outsider to be involved in a criminal activity of the Camorra was, in Izzo's recollection, not something that happened very often and not something that he relished happening. He recalled that there had been the occasional incident where the Camorra had assisted terrorists, but that had not happened for many years.

"Are you there?" the Englishman asked.

"I am here. Sorry for my, how do you say, ah yes – quietness."

"You are the inspector responsible for organized crime in the area?"

"No, I am responsible for investigating organized crime in the area." The AC in his turn held the receiver away from his ear and frowned. Was that not what I said, he thought?

"I was given your name and number by a superior."

"Who, please?" Pietro asked.

"General Barberini told me I should..."

Izzo interrupted, "No, no, I mean what is your name?"

"Oh, I am sorry, I should have said immediately. I'm Assistant Commissioner Bond of the Specialist Operations division of the Metropolitan Police Service in London."

"Ah yes, related to James?"

The ACSO was about to respond that James was his father when he realized the Italian police officer was attempting to crack a joke. "Yes, I see. Ha, ha, very funny." Normally Bond would have erupted in a tirade against such immaturity, but on this occasion, he needed a favour from the foreigner, and so swallowed it and moved on.

"I am terribly sorry to trouble you, Inspector, but we seem to have an organized crime situation brewing that is likely to affect your area. Part of my job is to handle organized crime. As part of an ongoing operation, one of my Detective Sergeants is driving down to Naples and will need your assistance. Your General seemed very keen to help."

The Englishman went on to explain the circumstances of the ongoing operation and how he felt that Izzo might best be of service, which amounted to keeping out of the way and letting the police officer who was due to arrive do his own thing. When Izzo replaced the telephone, he sat frowning at it for several minutes. He was so confused that he even forgot to worry his paperclips. He was just leaning over to pick up the telephone and dial the Colonel's extension when there was a smart rap on the door and the Colonel walked into the office.

"Izzo, how are you today?" he asked with a broad smile.

The Inspector sat back in his chair and smiled. The Colonel was a Black Cat, not unlike the one he had to deal with on the morning of the double murder. The Inspector had been about to call and ask this very man if he had heard of or from the English senior police officer. For him to arrive in the office at precisely that moment could not be a coincidence. He was more or less sure that he had not seen his boss for more than a month, and never in the office in Pozzuoli. Izzo had an office at the regional headquarters in the city centre, but preferred the Pozzuoli office, because it was not only central to his beat, but the seafront boasted some excellent seafood restaurants where he could go for lunch.

"I was at the Naval Base in Nisida and thought I would call over for a chat." Ah, not the Englishman, then, Izzo thought. "It seems the Colonel on the base is a little upset by your antics the other morning." Izzo could not recall his Commanding Officer ever having taken an interest in his day to day activities. This morning, it seemed, was a morning for firsts.

"I am investigating a double murder and needed some cooperation," he explained patiently. His CO was not known for a quick uptake.

"Quite right, that is what I told the Colonel." Ah, so it *is* the Englishman then, Izzo thought.

"Izzo, a situation has arisen with our English colleagues in The Met." Izzo wondered if the Colonel even knew what The Met was, but doubted it.

Chapter 7

The one-thousand-four-hundred-mile slog from Gloucester to Pozzuoli had been long and hard. The Fiat was not designed for long-distance driving even for smaller people with all their limbs hail. As he had been packing a bag in the Peckham apartment, Thumper considered buying a ticket on a Monarch charter flight out of Luton. He quickly realized, though, that he did not have the funds to pay for a flight and hire a car. The boss said he would be reimbursed for his expenses, but the initial outlay was all Thumper's. With Layla away at bridge for the weekend, the cards would already be stretched to their limits and hiring a car would not be an option. He knew he would not be able to run an investigation without a car. It meant having to drive a long distance in the pink monstrosity, but he could see no other way.

He boarded a late-night hovercraft out of Dover and began the arduous drive through France in the early hours of Monday morning. The journey had been slow, but after the sun had risen, was punctuated with some of the most beautiful scenery and awful tasting slop that Thumper had ever eaten. He had, of course, heard about the strange habit the French had of eating snails, but seeing them in the shell as it were, in a motorway service stop had been enough to put him off his breakfast and later his lunch. The further south he got, the stranger the food became, so in the end he was surviving on black coffee and nerves. When he crossed the border down by Chamonix, he was glad to arrive in Italy so he could get normal human food, edible stuff like spaghetti and pizza. He was disappointed though, because what he actually found on the Italian A1 motorway, which ran down the middle of the country like a spinal column, was that the motorway services were basic, offering fast food like burgers and chips, rather than the more sophisticated Italian fare like pizza and spaghetti. Still, anything was an improvement on the snails that the French had offered.

He arrived in the small town of Pozzuoli on the Tuesday morning, having driven through the night. He was at least grateful the one-way traffic system led right by the police station, so he was not reduced to searching for it. He parked the car and entered the run-down, sand coloured building with bars on the windows down the sides and a park full of palm trees at the front. The woman behind the desk told him she was a Brigadier in just passable English, before she took his details and showed him to an office beyond a sealed and coded door. He was still wondering at the woman's claim about being a Brigadier when she was obviously just a desk Sergeant, when she knocked on the door, opened it and ushered him in.

"Inspector, this man is Dee Ess T'umpa!" she said, before leaving and closing the door.

The office was small and claustrophobic, with no natural light. There was a filing cabinet, a rickety metal desk and two rickety metal chairs. The chair opposite the desk was occupied by a man in stark contrast to his surrounds.

"Inspector Izzo?" he asked while looking at the dapper little copper smoking a foul-smelling cigarette. He could see a pile of mangled paperclips on the desk and an overflowing ashtray of spent butts.

"No, no, it is I T S O, not I Z Z O."

"Oh, sorry about that. I wrote it down when she read it out to me and it is definitely spelt I Z Z O. Well, according to the ACSO's PA anyway."

"Do not trouble yourself," the Inspector waved a dismissive hand, which left a small column of smoke rings rising. "What is axos pee eh?"

"Axos what?"

"Just now, you said the axos pee eh."

"Oh, ACSO, the Assistant Commissioner Specialist Operations, his secretary."

"Sit down, please." Izzo indicated the chair opposite the desk. To Thumper it looked frail and creaked alarmingly when he lowered his bulk into it.

"Your AXO says you are carrying a gun." Thumper nodded.

"You must give it to me."

"I cannot do that. I am not authorised to surrender my weapon to anyone without the written consent of my firearms officer."

"I cannot have, forgive me, an alien policeman, walking about the city with a gun. It is against rules. I must follow rules." Thumper guessed that by alien the dapper Inspector did not mean a little green man with huge almond-shaped black eyes. He frowned, but eventually conceded the point and handed over his weapon.

"You will sign the form, yes? And we will return the weapon when you leave." Thumper nodded and signed the form. The firearms officer would shoot him if he found out, but the DS knew he would never find out, not unless he told him himself.

"Now, we go to early lunch and discuss your operation. You like seafood, yes?"

Thumper nodded, even though he did not know what Izzo meant by seafood. At least it would not be snails, he realized with some relief. As they left the office, the DS hoped the inspector meant fish and chips.

They walked a short distance to the seafront and Izzo waved Thumper into a chair at a table outside a small establishment. A waiter bustled over and poured two glasses of sparkling water without uttering a syllable and handed them both menus, that Izzo ignored. He began talking to the waiter at pace, while gesticulating frantically. Had it not been for the calmness of the waiter, Thumper would have thought that they were arguing. After the waiter left, Izzo waved in the general direction of the police station and asked, "That is your car, the rose one?"

"Rose?"

"Oh, I am sorry, the pink one? Rose is pink in Italian. I forget each time." Thumper expected some sort of ridicule when he nodded, turning a shade not unlike the colour of the car.

"It is a good Italian car," the inspector said. The DS could see no sign of mirth in the man's face and felt slightly relieved.

"Why are there so many derelict houses?" Thumper asked, thinking of all the boarded-up or simply crumbling buildings he had seen since arriving in the town.

"It was the earthquake, in eighty-three. No one has the money to fix the damage, so they remain like that. It is sad. There are people still living in, how do you say, cardboard houses?"

"Prefabs?" Thumper guessed.

"Yes, prefabs. I have ordered for you, yes?" Thumper nodded and hoped that the meal would be at least edible when it arrived.

As Thumper and Izzo were eating a grilled octopus and sea snail salad and discussing how they were going to cooperate with Thumper's investigation, Commander Willett and Assistant Commissioner Bond were in the AC's club in Soho eating Eggs Benedict as a late breakfast or an early brunch, and sipping espresso doppios, the latest rage in coffee to assault the city.

AC Bond was not in a very forgiving mood. After he had spoken to Willett the previous morning, he decided he would like some clarification and asked his PA to arrange this breakfast meeting.

"As I was saying, Dugs gave his man the green light on Sunday afternoon, so he should already be there, in," Willett consulted his notes, "Pozzuoli."

"Dugs?"

"Superintendent Douglas."

"Yes, I gathered that. What I meant was, why is he called Dugs?"

"Have you ever seen him with his uniform jacket off?" Willett asked with a chuckle.

The AC thought back, but could not recall having seen Douglas in his shirt sleeves. "I have seen him in a tux. Why?"

"It won't show in a tux. If you ever see him in his shirt sleeves, he has the biggest pair of…" Willett held his cupped hands in front of his chest for emphasis, but the Assistant Commissioner did not allow him to continue.

"Okay, Willett, I get the picture. Now, tell me what has been going on. I want the detail. I don't want you glossing over anything you consider to be unsavoury. Clear?" The AC knew that even with this encouragement, it was unlikely he would get the full story. Bad news not travelling up was as much a scientific certainty as shit storms travelling down.

"Yes, sir. Clear as crystal."

Willett proceeded to tell the AC about some of what had happened since the incident in Roper's. Bond already had a second-hand account of what happened in the club from the Home Secretary, because Roger Roper was a first cousin of the Secretary's wife. But the rest was sketchy. After the Home

Secretary called him, he had handed the problem off to Willett, with the assumption that his executive team would be able to clean up the mess. He had not expected to hear anything more about it, but when he received a call from Willett early on Monday morning, realized his assumption had been misplaced.

The Assistant Commissioner sat quietly, seeming to have more interest in his eggs than in what the Commander was saying about the case that was being built against the bodyguard who had assaulted a DS. Bond showed no interest in the department fabricating a case against Moses as some sort of face saving exercise. That is, until Willett reached the part about the bodyguard apparently searching for the son of a lawyer, one Christopher Alliss. The AC interrupted with a fork of Eggs Benedict half way to his mouth and a frown on his face.

"What, the son of Philip Alliss?"

"Yes, that is correct, sir. It seems that for some reason Moses is after the younger Alliss. Dugs seems to think it can be for no good at all. He thinks that this will provide his department with some traction in the case."

Assistant Commissioner Bond frowned at the egg on his fork. Willett would not know it, he was not party to the other division activities in the SO, but Philip Alliss was a person of interest. Only those who attended the weekly Executive Status meetings would be privy to that information. Them and Commander Blythe, Willett's peer in SO7, the branch responsible for investigating serious and organized crime, who had presented a report to the executives two weeks previously in which the lawyer was implicated in an ongoing investigation. Bond had not been paying attention on that morning, because he was reading the monthly budget report and only half listening. He had, however, caught the name Philip Alliss who was somehow connected to a crime syndicate and that he was father to Christopher Alliss.

"Go on." Bond encouraged Willett to continue his briefing, although he no longer paid any attention to what the Commander was saying. He had other, more pressing information to digest and react to.

"Keep me informed," he told Willett as soon as his eggs were finished. He left the Commander staring in his wake in bemusement as he left the club.

Back at his desk, Assistant Commissioner Bond pressed his intercom, "Margery, get Commander Blythe for me would you."

"Yes, sir."

Commander Blythe was in the AC's office within the hour sipping a dry sherry.

"I want the details, Derek. I need to know what the hell is going on with this Alliss chap and how in the hell we think this Moses fellow is involved." Blythe nodded and composed himself before starting.

"You know of course about our agreements with GCHQ and sundry bodies of a similar bent throughout Europe?" The AC nodded. "Well, one of the functions of the multiple listening stations is to notify the different law enforcement agencies when they pick up something of interest. Usually, the trigger is certain keywords, like bomb or assassination, but the listeners can also target known individuals." The Commander hesitated to allow the AC to digest what he was hearing.

"Go on."

"Several of those keywords were picked up by a listening station on the US Naval base in Naples in a mobile telephone conversation between a suspected member of a major crime syndicate around Naples and a leader of the Nuova Brigata Rossa, the Italian New Red Brigade a known..."

"I thought the Red Brigade was quashed in the eighties?" Bond interrupted.

"Yes, sir, it was. This is an offshoot of the original Brigata Rossa. The original crew went too far when they kidnapped and killed Aldo Moro. The whole country united against them, and in particular, the organized crime families." The Commander described how the various syndicates throughout Italy helped law enforcement agencies to track down the terrorists, and how that led to reprisals.

"The Red Brigade were responsible for several high-profile killings of Camorra and other Mafia organizations during that rift, but eventually they were crushed.

The New Red Brigade was created by some of the survivors of the original organization. As far as we can tell, they have not committed any crimes yet, but are under observation, hence the intercepted call."

"Why is the call pertinent?"

"A known member of a Neapolitan crime syndicate offered the NRB, and I quote 'one of our best soldiers'."

Again, the AC interrupted, "Let me guess, Christopher Alliss?"

"Yes, sir."

"So, we are seeing a lot of loose threads that all seem to originate from the same ball of string?"

"Yes, sir."

"And we are sure they are all connected?"

"Yes, sir. There seems to be a common theme." The Commander took a sip of his sherry to compose himself.

"Pray continue," the AC said.

"As you know, one of the remits of SO7 is counter terrorism, so GCHQ contacted the division with information regarding the intercepted call."

"Okay, so how do we fit in?"

"GCHQ contacted us because they wanted to know if we had any known terrorists or OC members of that name. We found no such records, but on a little further digging, we discovered that we have a national called Christopher Alliss who is the son of a Philip Alliss, a respected city lawyer…"

"How did we conclude that they are connected?" Bond interrupted.

"Philip Alliss was previously known as Filippo Elenco and is originally from the Naples region of Italy."

"Aha, so the plot thickens."

"Yes indeed. And now that the Detective Sergeant has chased this Moses character to Naples, we can surmise that somehow there is a connection."

"So, why do you think this Moses character is chasing down the Alliss boy?"

"I don't know why, but I like it. I don't believe in coincidence. There can be no coincidence in this case. As I said, it is all connected somehow, we just need to work out how. We can start with why would a bodyguard be on the hunt for the Alliss boy from a personal perspective? He would not. His beef is with The Met, not the lawyer. My guess is that he was hired by Philip Alliss."

"Yes, I think you are right. How are we containing Alliss?"

"We have the Alliss residence in Kensington under surveillance, but other than that, I think we should sit on our hands and wait for developments. It seems to me that Moses is tenacious and is likely to find the boy. After that is achieved, then we can decide how to proceed."

"I agree."

Chapter 8

Thumper sat on the bed in the cheap hotel and gazed down at the Glock sitting on top of the luggage in his backpack. He knew how the gun got there, that was obvious; he had the pack at the restaurant by the seafront. Having the bag with him was force of habit as much as anything. Living in Peckham, he never left anything in the car and so did the same in Pozzuoli, despite it being parked next to a police station. He also took the pack with him when they left for lunch, rather than have to go back for it. The Italian detective must have slipped the weapon into it when he was in the karsi throwing up the octopus and sea snail salad.

It seemed that the charade about him giving up his weapon had been on behalf of whoever it was in charge and needed to see all the dots and crosses in their correct places. Thumper was confused about the motives of the dapper copper. Why would he give him back his firearm? It seemed a little odd in the circumstances. It felt better to have it though, safer somehow, although he had no clue as to why he felt safer. He had never fired it at another human, only at the targets on the range. You could stick as many black and white images of assassins on wooden targets as you wanted, they were still only paper, plywood and glue. He slipped the weapon into the shoulder holster that was hanging on the back of the chair beside the bed before falling into a fitful sleep while fully dressed.

The same evening that DS Thumper sat on his bed in a cheap hotel in Pozzuoli wondering about the motives of the dapper copper, Archie was in the Philips Hotel in Eindhoven cradling a Jenever and contemplating a cheap print of Van Gogh's Sunflowers on the wall above the minibar. He had hired a car and taken the overnight ferry from Harwich to the Hoek of Holland. The drive down through the flat countryside of the Netherlands had been uneventful, with nothing more interesting to look at than the occasional windmill.

During the drive, Archie had time to think about where his life was going, and where it had been. He was not really one for reminiscing, preferring to keep eyes to the front, but the events of recent days caused him to look back and to think. The retro-thinking continued while he was checking in and after he let himself into the hotel room. He poured a couple of mini-bottle measures of the Dutch gin from the bar, and wondered what fate had driven him to be sitting on an expensively bought bed in a continental city chasing a target in which he had no interest.

Sure, there was the orphanage, but he did not like to think about that. It was a time of his life he would rather forget. That he had never known his mother did not bother him. What you never had, you cannot miss, right? But what really led to his current predicament was his army days. When they had had enough of him at the Sisters of Mercy, they turfed him out into the Army Cadets in Aldershot. He supposed it was meant as some sort of punishment, but he had never been happier than when he was in the army.

After he arrived in Aldershot, Archie's lot became a little easier, despite his Non-Commissioned superiors not reacting well to his presence. He was a very intelligent kid and should probably have gone to Sandhurst for officer cadet training, but coming from an underprivileged background, that would never happen. The NCOs were in a different category from Archie. They were still gutter trash, but they had been elevated to superiority through an ability to say "yes, sir" without showing any negative emotion, as well as a demonstrable disregard for their fellow men. The Corporals and Sergeants saw him as a threat to their status quo. Unfortunately for them, Archie was more or less immune to what they considered to be the best method of treatment for 'wayward' cadets. Sticking their noses in his face and shouting obscenities about his mother was as effective as giving him hot chocolate and biscuits and sending him to bed. The NCOs in the academy spent two years from his sixteenth to his eighteenth trying to break him. If any of the MoD's bean counters had bothered to study the statistics, they would have seen a marked rise in the transfer requests of Cadet School training NCOs over that same two-year period.

When he reached his eighteenth birthday, Archie had the option to sign on with the adult army, or leave and seek his fortune in the public sector. It surprised everyone except Archie himself when he chose to sign on for a twenty-two-year stretch. What the army careers personnel failed to consider during his pre-passing-out consultations was how he had fit in with his peers in the cadets. Most of those sixteen year olds ended up in Aldershot because they were unwanted somewhere else. They were all misfits for one reason or another, and for the first time in his life, Archie was not the odd one out.

Despite having spent two years training with the cadets, Archie had to redo his basic training when he joined the Royal Greenjackets. During basic training in 'The Sweeps', he was noticed for the first time as perhaps someone who might be very well suited to the life of extreme violence, which was the normal lot of a soldier. His strength and mental agility meant that he excelled both in the physical and the academic. He became known as a leader of men, not because he wanted others to succeed, but because he did not want the members of his unit to hold him back in any way. He would often be seen on the assault course helping others over obstacles, or in the classroom, helping others with particularly difficult academic problems. He passed out of basic training as top of the class in every respect.

Archie's superiority over his peers continued after he became a proper soldier. Aided by the same mental and physical agility he demonstrated in basic training, Archie made Lance Corporal in record time. It was also in record time that he was recommended for a more active role in the family of the British Army and was put forward for the Special Air Service (SAS) selection process. There was no hardship for Archie when it came to the trials in the Brecon Beacons. He climbed the mountains and did the runs and was noticed by the selectors as a cut above the rest of the two hundred or so candidates, which was unusual, because most of them came from the paras or commandos and were not known for their lack of physical fitness. It was during the rest of the five-week selection process that it all came crashing down. As an orphan, Archie had never been anywhere near an airplane. As part of the SAS selection process he was expected to jump from a rather large airplane with the other candidates in his selection unit. He was in line shuffling forward towards the open maw of the Hercules troop carrier twenty-thousand feet somewhere above the British Isles when his fear of heights manifested itself. He refused to go anywhere near the rear doors and was so strong that none of the trainers in the plane could compel him to jump. They might have succeeded had they ganged up on him, but protocol forbade them to throw anyone out of a plane, however much they might want to.

Archie's SAS career ended before it even began.

What use a trooper in a branch of the armed services that put as much emphasis on the air bit as the special bit? What use a trooper who could not halo jump into a hotspot and blow away the enemies of the state if they could not face the open maw of a Hercules troop carrier? Archie was RTUd (returned to unit) with a note on his file saying that he would be a very adept soldier so long as the conflict was contained within England, Wales or Scotland or a ship was the method of delivery to the respective theatre. That SAS trial and note on his file condemned Archie to a military career confined to an HQ somewhere in England where he would be sitting behind a desk doing administrative work. Any type of work that did not require his presence wherever the regiment were at any given moment: he ended up as a payroll clerk answering enquiries from aggrieved soldiers in the field.

It was only a matter of time before Archie lashed out. When it came, the lash was aimed at a particularly annoying recently graduated Second Lieutenant who walked around the call centre making sure that the troops did not abuse the telephones they used to answer enquiries. Archie was honourably discharged (no one wanted to prosecute him for striking a superior considering the circumstances of the offence) and he took up a job as a bodyguard, recommended to the post by one of the SAS selectors who had noted his ability during the three-day Brecon Beacon trials.

Archie quaffed the glass of Jenever and turned off his bedside light. Despite it being only ten thirty, he felt tomorrow would be a long day and he would benefit from a good night's sleep.

Chapter 9

The next afternoon, Archie was sitting in the hire car in a car park on Wilhelminaplein near to Eindhoven city centre. After checking out of the hotel that morning, he went to the railway station and bought a tour guide of the city. He looked up the restaurant while drinking coffee in the station café. Le Pied de Cochon unsurprisingly, specialized in French gourmet cuisine and he decided to give it a try. Archie ate a lunch of a garlic snail starter, wild boar with dauphinoise potatoes for the main and a crème brulee for desert before asking to speak to the owner who, if the travel guide was accurate, was a certain Jan van den Hemmel.

When he was ushered into the office above the kitchen he could tell that the owner thought him there either to complain about the service or as a restaurant critic. The very tall and slightly portly man seemed to be fuming behind his ornate desk. That impression was exaggerated by his waxed handlebar moustaches.

"Bonjour," he said, falsely pronouncing the jay as a why. "How may I help?" with a look that carried the opposite sentiment.

Archie stifled a laugh. The man was obviously affecting a Frenchness that had more to do with profit-making than with his origins.

"I am looking for a missing person, one Christopher Alliss."

"That bastar'," the man blustered.

"How so," Archie asked? It seemed to be turning into a common theme with all those that Alliss had met. Reading between rather flowery expletives, Archie gathered that Christopher's lack of classical training had been immediately apparent to the chef du restaurant.

"The advertisement specifically requested a classical training. 'Ee thought me an idiot that I would not know 'eem as a charlatan."

"How did you know?" Archie was somewhat baffled by his own question. Why did he care how the pompous restaurateur with a false French accent knew that the Alliss boy was a fake? It made no difference to the job in hand. None.

""Ee could not even make a parmesan tuile for the risotto." Archie frowned. A parmesan tuile? Risotto?

"'Ee did not survive the first dinner sitting before I sacked 'eem." This latest accompanied with a very Italian gesture involving a bent elbow and an extended middle finger. Archie wondered about the gesture and why there was risotto and parmesan tuiles on the menu of a gourmet French restaurant owned by a man with a fake accent and a very Dutch name, but let it drop.

"The man is a fake, a charlatan." The owner reiterated. "If you find 'eem, tell 'eem I said so."

"I will tell him. Do you have a forwarding address?" met with a Gallic shrug.

"No, I did hear though, 'ee was drinking in Kaffee De Groot down on Wilhelminaplein. You might try there."

And so Archie was looking at the bar from the driver seat of his hire car. He found the square depressing. Now, even in the height of summer, there was a battleship grey feeling about the place, despite the exterior décor being colourful, and different for each of the bars that fronted the car park. Kaffee De Groot (The Cave) was to the right of where Archie had parked the car. He climbed out and made his way into the narrow bar. The interior was dark. Archie waited a few moments for his eyes to adjust. He saw a couple of men on barstools drinking Dutch beer flutes of Pils to his right and a tall slim man behind the bar with a scar on his left cheek, polishing glasses with a tea-towel. The drinkers stopped their conversation in mid-flow as Archie walked in.

"Can I help?" the barman asked with an Irish accent.

Archie walked over and showed him the photo of Chris Alliss. "Have you seen this boy?"

The Irishman did not look at the photo, just responded. "No, never saw him before," before picking up a clean beer flute and polishing it. The two men at the bar returned to their conversation, affecting an air of nonchalance meant as a dismissal.

Archie nodded and smiled. "His father is desperately looking for information about him. The boy has been missing for months and he's worried."

The barman nodded and frowned, but still did not look at the photo. Archie guessed that motivation for his reticence was probably financial, so he took his wallet out of his pocket.

"Keep yer feckin' geld, I ain't a grass!" the Irishman exploded before Archie could offer him any money.

"I am sure you're not a grass. Look, what's your name."

The barman looked around at the patrons, as if asking their advice on whether to impart the information. They looked at him with non-comital expressions. After hesitating for a few seconds, he reluctantly answered. "Mick."

"Well, Mick, let's have a drink. How about a Jenever?" Again, the barman hesitated. "A glass of Jenever doesn't mean squat, does it?"

Mick nodded and poured two of the Dutch gins. As they sipped the oily liquid, Archie approached the subject of Chris. "I know you are not a grass Mick, but I am not a copper. I'm actually a bodyguard." Archie took out his business card and handed it over. The Irishman still seemed wary.

"If yer a bodyguard, why're you lookin' for the boy?"

"I am doing it as a favour to his father."

"How do I know yer not a copper?"

"You will just have to take me at face value. But I swear to you I am not a copper."

"What's his name, the boy?"

"Chris Alliss."

Mick waved his hand at the photograph. Archie handed it over and the barman looked at it for long moments before answering. "I didn't know him well. Just knew him to see, an' took him home one night after too many scoops. He was in here a few times a week, a month or so back."

"How did he seem to you?" The question was out before Archie had time to consider it. Why the hell did he ask that?

"I dunno, he was nervous about summat, I guess."

"What makes you say that?"

"His drinking. He didn't drink like an alco, not measured like, but quaffed it down like he was trying to forget something."

Archie frowned. Something had changed in the dynamic of this task he had undertaken under duress. He was supposed to be tracking the boy, not investigating his mood swings. All he was supposed to do was locate him, report it back to the smarmy lawyer, and then get back to work protecting those with lots of money and no need of protection.

"He was hanging around with some shady eyeties, too. I didn't know them either."

"Shady how?"

"Deffo they were dodgy. I've hung around with dodgy characters before. I know what they feel like. Armani suits and don't take their shades off indoors. Even in here. Pair of 'em bumped into that table on their way out," he said, indicating a small table in the bar area.

"Would you know them again?" Know them again, Archie frowned. He was even beginning to sound like a copper to himself. What the hell did that mean anyway, would you know them again? It was like a bad line out of Hawaii Five O.

"Yeah, sure. But they stopped comin' here even before your boy."

"So, they arrived after Chris and left before him?"

"Yeah, deffo. It was like he brought them here."

"I don't suppose you know where he went?"

"No, but he lived in a Pension, a Bee and Bee round on Heilige Geeststraat. I know cos', like I said, I helped him back one night after a few too many Jenevers."

"Is it far?"

"No, next street over from the bar. Fourth door down on the right."

Five minutes later Archie was knocking on the door of the bed and breakfast where Alliss had stayed the month before. A little old man answered on the third knock and broke immediately into English.

"How can I help you?" Archie was bemused that everyone in this city knew immediately that he was an Englishman, or at least English-speaking.

"Is it that obvious?" he asked.

"Is what obvious?"

"That I am English."

"Yes, yes, obvious. Now how can I help? You need a room? Twenty-five a night. One night in advance." The man seemed to be in a hurry and not willing to be dealing with intrusions at this time of the day.

Archie shook his head. "I am inquiring after a guest who stayed here for a little while about a month ago, give or take."

"What was his name?"

"Chris Alliss."

"Ah yes, that boy. He still owes for two nights. You will pay for two nights? Fifty Guilders." Archie agreed to pay and the man's demeanour became much less hostile. "Come in, I will make you tea."

The old man led him into a dingy room that smelt vaguely of cats and had a carpet on the table. He left to make tea and returned a short while later.

"Sit," he said. As they sat drinking the insipid tea, Archie asked for information about the Alliss boy. "You pay, then we talk."

Archie handed over a fifty guilder note and then smiled encouragement for the man to tell him what he knew.

"He was troubled boy. Very nervous."

"Did you ever discover why he was nervous, sir?"

"Call me Arrie, sir makes me old." Archie smiled. Arrie *was* old. It seemed obvious that he was old enough to have witnessed the bombing of Eindhoven during the war, when the city was flattened by the USAAF and the RAF. "No, we never discovered and then he just left. One morning he didn't come for boiled eggs and cheese. I looked for him the next day, but he was gone."

"You have no idea why he left?"

"No, I packed away a box of his things in case he returns, do I show them to you?" Archie nodded.

Some short while later he was standing at Arrie's carpeted table laying out the contents of the box, piece by piece. There was nothing of much value, or importance. A cinema ticket stub; a folded sheet of writing paper, which when unfolded turned out to be the letter Chris had written to Ann the teacher. There was a brown smear across the writing that looked remarkably like a skid mark. Archie shook his head. The girl said that she had returned the letter, she failed to mention that she had wiped her arse with it first. The final piece of the detritus that marked the Alliss boy's passing through the drab city of Eindhoven was a postcard. It was a black and white postcard of a sleepy fishing village, which Archie guessed was somewhere in Italy. He flipped it over. The message was very short. "Come immediately. Take the train. Talk to no one." It was not signed, the only clue to the whereabouts of the sender was the postmark, which was for a town called Pozzuoli in the Province of Naples.

Chapter 10

The drive down through France and Italy in early summer was a pleasant enough experience for Archie. He did not feel any need for haste and stopped frequently en route to sample the exquisite French cuisine. He was a great fan of gourmet cookery and there was nowhere better to sample it than where it originated. He even took a short detour off the motorway to visit Lyon, because he had heard so much about the city's excellent food. When he crossed the border into Italy, his culinary journey continued, because to some, the Northern Italian cuisine could rival that of France. Archie was not sure which he preferred, but that was an indecision he felt would require endless investigation to resolve.

After Eindhoven, he had resigned himself to the reality of his Odyssey, realizing there was no benefit to be gained from fretting over where the job was taking him. He had not given it much thought before checking out of the Philips hotel and heading south through France.

He arrived in the town of Pozzuoli during the early evening of the Thursday after the chase had begun. He bought a tour guide at the station and selected a hotel down by the seafront. The hotel receptionist asked for his passport when he booked into the hotel. He did not feel any reluctance to hand it over, vaguely aware of some law that required passport checks for each hotel in the regions that were under the sway of the French during the Napoleonic conflict.

"When will I get it back?"

"Tomorrow. The border police will register it tonight and return it in the morning."

Archie nodded and went up to his room. The drive, although pleasant, had taken a lump out of him and he felt suddenly very tired. He threw off his clothes, crawled under the white cotton sheet and fell into a deep sleep within a minute of his head hitting the pillow.

He slept through the night without interruption and felt wholly refreshed on the Friday morning when he awoke after ten o'clock to the sound of dense traffic below his open window. Archie dressed and went down for something to eat. There were two uniformed police officers talking to the receptionist, so Archie stood beside them and waited to ask where he could get his breakfast.

The receptionist interrupted one of the police officers and asked, "How can I help?"

"Breakfast?"

"What is your room number?"

"Twenty-three." He saw a barely perceptible nod from the receptionist and then felt his arms jerked up behind his back. One of the police officers said something to the receptionist, who translated for Archie.

"You are under arrest." Archie nodded. He had been able to gather that much on his own.

"What is the charge?" He asked. The receptionist spoke rapidly to the officers.

"No charge yet, sir. You are, how do you say, helping policemen with their investigation." That confused him somewhat. If there was no charge, then why were his hands cuffed behind his back and why had the man said he was under arrest?

The officers marched him out to a blue and white Alpha Romeo and shuffled him into the back, making sure to bang his head on entering. A short time later Archie found himself for the second time in a matter of days in an interview room with his wrist shackled to the chair on which he was sitting. The only real difference was the heat and a lack of a neon flicker. While being frogmarched through the police station, Archie noticed that the other rooms and even the corridors had air conditioning. He guessed the lack of any in the interview room was not an oversight.

A uniformed police officer asked him in halting English if he wanted anything and brought him the bottle of still water he requested. Archie took a swig and sat back to wait. He had waited only a few minutes when the door opened and a short, dapper man walked in smoking a foul-smelling cigarette.

"They'll kill you, you know," Archie said, not expecting the man to understand.

"I know, for many years I have wished to give up, but I can't stand the smell of blood." Archie was not sure he understood how smoking would play a role in the detective's haemophobia.

The man smiled and sat down. "Let me introduce myself. I am Inspector Izzo of the DIA."

"What, like the drug squad?" Archie interrupted. The Inspector smiled again and shook his head.

"No, it stands for Direzione Investigativa Antimafia."

"So, the anti-mafia squad then?" Archie asked.

The Italian police officer nodded.

"What the hell do you want with me? I've got no connection with the Mafia, either here or at home."

Despite the frustrated tone of the question, Archie had relaxed somewhat. He now guessed that his arrest was a simple case of mistaken identity and he might be on his return journey by the end of the day, so long as locating the boy turned out not to be difficult. He assumed that it would not be too hard, as the town was small and the boy would almost certainly be working in a restaurant. It would be just a case of visiting them one by one until he found him.

"You are Archibald Moses?" Archie nodded. "We received a tip from The Met in London that you were coming here. We were told that you are involved with a crime syndicate and that a crime is taking place."

Okay, *not* mistaken identity then, Archie laughed as he thought. He could not help but laugh. He had compared The Met with characters from a Blake Edwards plot, what with a giant man chasing him to Gloucester in a pink car and a plaster cast. He had seen the copper outside The Cock 'n Bull in Gloucester looking indecisive, but the man had not given chase from there. Archie thought he must have realized the futility of it and stopped. Now he guessed differently. Somehow the police officer had uncovered information about where Archie was going before Archie knew himself. There had been no sign of the car since Gloucester. It would have been easy to spot if the tail had resumed. There was no pink Fiat in Eindhoven, or on the trip down from Eindhoven, or indeed in Pozzuoli.

"You find the situation funny?" the Inspector inquired. However, the smile did not leave his face; Archie found it disconcerting. He had been in similar situations on many occasions, the latest being in The Yard only a few days before, but never had he seen the interrogators smiling so genuinely and for such a length of time.

"Yes, hilarious, actually."

"Why?"

"I was falsely arrested in London a few days ago, and now I am here, falsely arrested again at the behest, seemingly, of the same fuckers who did it before." Archie attempted to return the man's smile but it came out as a grimace.

Izzo looked at his suspect. He did not really suspect him of anything. The man did not appear to be the type who would be involved with the Camorra. Not only was he extremely white, not the olive colour usually associated with the local organized crime syndicate, but he had an air of competence and a confidence in his current situation that would be unusual in a guilty man.

"You are not under arrest, Mr Moses." The Inspector was letting Moses know that he had not fallen for the story The Met tried to spin. It did not seem plausible and he knew that something else was probably happening. When he met the police officer from the Organized Crime unit, a tall and handsome man with big muscles and no brains, he was wholly convinced the Assistant Commissioner had lied to him. Or if not lied, then at least had not told him or his seniors a complete story.

What he agreed with the blond officer over lunch, was that he would stay out of the investigation. He knew when he agreed with the man that it was a lie and he would apprehend this Archibald Moses, if only to discover what his London counterparts were doing. Izzo did not like being taken for a fool under any circumstances, but especially not when he was in his own back yard.

"Really, in case you hadn't noticed, I am shackled to a chair." Archie rattled his wrist for emphasis.

"Yes, I apologise about that, my subordinates are, how do you say, too keen?"

"Fanatical? Overzealous?" Archie prompted. "By the way, how did you know where I was?"

"I get a report from the border police each morning. Your name was flagged in the report. I asked for them to watch when the London police contacted me." The Inspector stretched his smile, if possible, and shouted for a guard.

When the uniformed officer entered the room, the inspector continued to shout at him until he had retrieved the handcuff key from his belt and released Archie's wrist from the manacles. Archie got the impression that it was a rehearsed scenario, a bit like the Italian version of 'good cop, bad cop'. When it was done, Izzo spread his arms wide, indicating Archie's freedom.

"Now, as I said, not arrested, helping with investigation." Archie did not find the gesture particularly conciliatory; he was still detained at the discretion of this little police detective.

"What do you want from me, Inspector?" he sighed.

"Easy, Mr Moses. I want to know why you are here."

"On holiday." Archie attempted. Now it was the turn of the inspector to laugh.

"Very funny. No, I think if that was true, The Met would not be showing so much interest."

Archie laughed again. "I'm guessing, Inspector, that you don't have much dealing with The Met." Izzo shook his head. "No, I guessed not. Their reasons can defy the simplest logic."

"So, you do not know why I am asked to help with an investigation by your London police?"

"No, Inspector, I don't."

Izzo was frustrated because an armed police officer was in his domain. He could have withheld the man's sidearm, but he knew how naked he would feel without a weapon and he did not want the man looking elsewhere to find a gun. He was also frustrated that this Archibald Moses seemed to have less idea than he did about what was going on. He could find himself in trouble with the Colonel, because arresting Moses was also something that had not been included in his orders form the Black Cat. Quite the reverse, the Colonel had ordered him to confiscate the police officer's weapon and then let him get on with whatever it was he wanted to get on with.

"Tell me a guess, Mr Moses, why the English Mafia police are after you."

"I wish I knew why The Met are after me, truly I do. All I know is that I hurt one of their officers defending my client in a club in Covent Garden."

"Your client, Mr Moses? What job is it that you do?"

"I am a bodyguard for celebrities. One of The Met officers attacked a client of mine in Roper's nightclub on Friday night and I defended her."

"Friday last week?"

"Yes."

The Inspector had no further doubts about this man's innocence. If it was an act, he was a very good actor. No, this Moses had no connection with the Camorra. The English police had lied for some reason. None of it made any sense.

"So again, Mr Moses, why are you here?"

"I am searching for a missing person."

"What missing person, please?"

Archie briefly considered stalling, but then realized it was a futile gesture. He owed nothing to Alliss and would tell the Inspector everything in the end, so why not save time and tell it immediately?

"His name is Christopher Alliss. He is the son of my client." Archie supposed that to be true. Alliss was paying for him to track down the boy, so that made him a client, if only technically.

"Why did you come to here?"

"I have reason to think that the Alliss boy is here."

"And why is he here in Pozzuoli?"

Archie shrugged. He had no idea why the Alliss boy might be in Pozzuoli. The postcard had been vague, but Archie suspected something sinister. The barman in Eindhoven had mentioned thuggish looking Italians in Ray-Bans and Armani suits and Archie was aware of the organized crime syndicates in the South of Italy. They had a reputation for being merciless. He hoped that the boy meeting Italians in Kaffee De Groot had been coincidence. This was meant to be a locate and report mission, not a rescue.

"You are sure you don't know why the boy is here?"

"I am sure. I followed him to a town in the Netherlands called Eindhoven, and from there I drove down to Pozzuoli."

The Inspector frowned his incomprehension. "Why did you not fly?"

Archie bristled slightly. He did not like to admit that he was afraid of flying. "I could only get a flight to Rome from Schiphol. By the time I'd driven to Amsterdam and then driven a car from Rome, I'd have been here already."

The inspector nodded his acceptance of the explanation and asked to see the postcard Archie had found in the bed and breakfast on Heilige Geeststraat. Izzo read it before looking at

Archie with a bemused expression. "Why was he supposed to come immediately?" Archie shrugged again.

"Do you have a photograph?"

Archie took the original photo that Alliss had given him and handed it over to the inspector. He could afford to give it away, because he had made several copies in a printing outlet in Gloucester as a precaution. At the time, he had berated himself as being too much of a fusspot, now he was glad he had done it. Izzo studied the photo intently for a few minutes before looking up at Archie with a triumphant expression.

"You are free to go."

"What, now?"

"Yes, free to go now." Izzo called the uniformed officer into the room and spoke to him in Italian. "Officer Greco will process you out."

With that the inspector nodded at Archie and left the room without so much as an apology for any inconvenience that might have been caused.

"Cipolle, with me," he shouted as he ran through the open plan office where his team generally sat waiting for the next murder to be discovered. The Sergeant was pinning evidence from the double homicide on the cork board at the front of the office space. He sighed and left the room after his boss. He did not run, but followed Izzo at a slow walk into the viewing room in the cellar of the station. When he entered the room the inspector was already playing the tape they had received from the naval base on Nisida. He paused the tape just as the unknown man lifted his face, as if he were a model making sure that his profile was facing the camera.

"Look," Izzo said, wafting the photo under Cipolle's nose. "It's him."

Cipolle looked at the photo and then nodded his agreement. It was the same person. "Who is he?"

"His name is Christopher Alliss."

Chapter 11

Discovering the identity of the man in the CCTV footage had made the Inspector's day. He had been worrying about it ever since the tape had arrived from the camp commandant with instructions to return it when the investigation was over. Izzo worried because the Camorra working with an outsider was not only very unusual, but would make all the normal lines of inquiry next to useless. Following the normal trail of very large breadcrumbs would just lead to a hungry magpie. The inspector smiled at the analogy as he climbed into the unmarked car parked at the back of the station.

Before leaving he made a few inquiries of his Alien's Police colleagues, those responsible for foreign nationals who take up residence in Italy. He had not really expected them to provide any information, but was surprised. It seemed that Christopher Alliss had registered his presence in the town upon arrival a few weeks previously. That would normally have confused Izzo. Why would someone involved in illegal activity register with the local police? As he drove, the inspector thought that he might have the answer. The riddle of why the bodies had been dumped on Nisida might also be resolved by the boy's action. Whatever was going on, the

Camorra needed a scapegoat. They had used the Alliss boy to dump the bodies so that his face would appear on camera. They could have dumped the bodies outside any military base in the region, knowing that the CCTV would work there and Christopher Alliss's inexperience would get him noticed.

The inspector doubted the boy had any involvement in the murders, and suspected they were unrelated. Quite possibly, punishment killings for some infringement of the Camorra's unwritten laws. The two bodies belonged to a Camorra clan from the region of Caserta: their identities had been known within a few hours of their bodies being discovered. Fingerprints, DNA, all had come back and corroborated the information. No, their deaths were coincidental to what Alliss was doing in the region.

Now that he knew who he was and where he was, Izzo felt he had two choices. He could arrest him and attempt to discover what was going on by interrogation, but he suspected that would not provide him with any information he could use against the Camorra. The locals would have been sure to cover their involvement in case the boy was apprehended for some reason. After all, it was possible, if not likely, that he would be recognized from the CCTV footage and apprehended immediately. Or he could follow him and discover what the Camorra family was up to. He opted for the latter approach without giving it too much consideration. It was obviously the best course of action.

Chris Alliss was registered as an under-chef in a seafood restaurant called 'La Orchidea' down the coast in Posillipo. 'La Orchidea' was a renowned restaurant and attracted clientele from all over the country. It was also a business front for a well-known Camorra family. Izzo's investigation had already taken a leap forward, even without any further traction he now knew which of the families was involved in the double murder. He was yet to discover why the two hoods from Caserta had been killed, but suspected that that information would become apparent during the investigation.

Before starting his engine, Izzo checked his watch. It was time for lunch and he had heard good things about the restaurant's seafood. He would try it and see.

Archie knew it would now be easy to find Christopher Alliss. He felt he could, after all, be driving back to London by the end of the day. As soon as the formalities were over and he was released from police custody and out of view of the station, Archie ran to the hotel. He did not go to his room, but returned to the back of the police station in the hire car. Finding Alliss would be a simple matter of following the detective.

Archie felt he would get back in time, because there would be some checking required before the inspector could leave. He just knew by the dapper little man's face that he also wanted Alliss. The way the detective reacted when he saw the photo left Archie with no doubt about what his next action would be. Archie had no idea why, but Chris Alliss was a person of interest.

He frowned as he waited in the parking spaces at the back of the station. His initial reticence to take on the job now seemed justified. There was more to this affair than the lawyer had let on. It was becoming complicated and Archie was going against his better instincts by not jacking it in and telling Alliss to take a leap.

Even before he was discharged from the police station, he had decided to wait and follow Izzo. He might be wrong and be led on a fox hunt, but he did not think so, with good reason. He did not have long to wait before he saw Izzo leave the station and climb into an unmarked car parked in the spaces on Maria Sacchini. He followed as the Inspector pulled out and drove through the town's one-way system before heading out onto the coast road.

He was not surprised when Izzo parked the car outside a restaurant in a place called Posillipo, a twenty-minute drive from Pozzuoli. The Inspector took a table under the awning at the front of the restaurant. A couple of hours later, Archie admitted that he was not really enjoying this transition from bodyguard to detective. Detective work seemed extremely boring. At least as a bodyguard he got to wear an earpiece and meet the rich and famous. He had watched Izzo sitting under the awning at the front of the restaurant eating a leisurely lunch, before ordering some sort of after-dinner drink and a coffee. The Italian seemed to be in no hurry, biding his time to make sure he had the right result, or just too engrossed in his lunch to be worried about catching the boy. Archie was beginning to wonder if his plan had been a false hope and whether he was indeed on a fox hunt. Maybe Izzo had not been interested in the photo, but just had a sudden pang to take an early and very long lunch?

Archie had almost accepted that conviction as reality by the middle of the afternoon, when two men left the restaurant and made their way towards a parked car. He could not see who the men were, but they got into the car and pulled out into traffic. At that moment, Inspector Izzo ran to his own vehicle so he could follow.

Archie started his engine and pulled out into traffic a few cars behind the two men. As they drove past Inspector Izzo, something in their posture told Archie that they knew he was there; they seemed to be very stiff and staring straight ahead, not unlike crash dummies. As he passed, he saw that a little old lady with a silver bun on top of her head had double parked and Izzo's unmarked car was boxed in. He watched the detective banging his fists on the steering wheel in frustration, and screaming at her. She just kept touching her ear and shaking her head. Archie thought her excuse was probably not true, because he was sure the dead would be able to hear the Inspector's screams, his patience of the morning and later while eating a leisurely lunch, seemed to have been evaporated by the summer heat.

Archie followed the car down the crowded coastal road and eventually onto the A3 motorway flyover. The two men were heading south out of the city. Archie did not know who was in the car, but decided the best way to confirm that one of them was the Alliss boy, was to follow and hope he could catch up when they got out of the car.

He was surprised some time later, when they pulled off the motorway and parked in the car park out the front of the excavations of Pompeii. He felt that a visit to the city smothered in ashes by a volcano some two thousand years previously was out of place. He was pulling into an available spot when the two men walked past him and headed for the main entrance to the site. He could see that one of the men was indeed Christopher Alliss.

As he left the car, Archie saw a bank of public telephones on the other side of the car park. He briefly thought about heading for the nearest one and calling Alliss Senior with information about the location of his son, so he could return to his normal life as a celebrity bodyguard. Alliss had asked him to locate the boy, which he had now done. There was no need for him to continue pretending to be a detective, not really. But something held him back. Something told him that the boy was in trouble and just like when he was in The Sweeps, Archie did not have it in him to abandon a person in need. When in the Green Jackets, he had convinced himself he was only furthering his career each time he helped one of his comrades, but that was self-deluding. He sighed, bought a ticket and followed them into the site.

He could just see them walking down what appeared to be the main thoroughfare of the excavations and ran to catch up. Running was difficult, because the road was rutted and had very large central stepping stones; he seemed to be jumping from stone to stone rather than running. He followed them as they turned to the right, and as he turned, he saw what appeared to be a small fortress within the city bounds. It was as he neared that he realized it was an amphitheatre. It looked like it had been built recently and abandoned for tax reasons, like so many other building projects in the Mediterranean.

He watched the two men make their way through the nearest arch. They were acting stealthily, constantly looking back to see if they were followed. Archie just looked like a tourist, so they ignored him. They were looking for Italians, specifically Italians with an aura of authority about them, an aura of police. He hurried his pace and ducked into the same corridor through which they had entered. After the glare of the afternoon sun, the shade under the arch seemed dense and impenetrable. Archie rushed forward and nearly ran into three men closeted under one of the corridor arches.

"Cazzo (dick)!" one of the men shouted.

Because Archie's eyes were becoming accustomed to the dim light, he could see the three men clearly. Two were obviously locals, with the deep olive skin most common in the area. The other was white. Archie ignored the olive-skinned men and spoke directly to the other. "Chris, Chris Alliss?"

"Who the fuck're you?" It seemed to Archie that the boy was trying to affect an air of hardness to impress whoever he was with. There was a tense atmosphere in the small group. Archie wondered if he had created it, or if it had been there before he arrived.

He smiled, trying to ease the tension. "Your father sent me. He is worried about you."

"Chris, who is this man?" one of the Italians asked.

Chris shrugged his shoulders. The other man, a youth with a white cotton summer suit, a baseball cap and Ray-Ban sunglasses, who looked to Archie to be in his late teens, smiled a dazzlingly bright-toothed smile and pulled a nine-millimetre semi-automatic pistol out of the waistband at the back of his trousers. Archie looked at the gun. It was like one of those he had seen in war films, big, metallic silver and threatening. The man grinned, shrugged, and pointed the weapon between Archie's eyes.

Chapter 12

Sergeant Cipolle was sitting at the communal desk in the open plan area looking at mug shots of well-known Camorriste when inspector Izzo stormed into the office with an obvious hornet up his arse. The Sergeant frowned when the inspector slammed the door to the reception area where waiting visitors were witnesses to his petulance. Cipolle could not remember his boss being so angry. He closed the folder of known thugs and sighed. He would have to continue to familiarize himself with them on another occasion.

The inspector kicked a waste paper basket across the room before screaming, "Cipolle, in my office now."

Unlike earlier when he had sauntered into the viewing room at the boss's request, the Sergeant ran to the office. Something had upset Izzo very badly and it was best not to squeeze lemon into the open wound.

"Yes, sir?" he asked as he entered the office.

"Close the door and sit down."

Cipolle sat in the rickety chair nearest the door, stretched out his legs, crossed his ankles and intertwined his fingers before placing his hands on his chest. He followed the same routine each time he sat down in front of a desk that carried an ashtray, especially one that was overflowing with spent butts. The routine was designed to prevent him from lighting a cigarette. It did not work too often, but at least he was trying.

"What's up, boss?" he asked, preparing himself for the inevitable tirade.

"Get that checked," Izzo threw a crumpled piece of paper onto the desk in front of the Sergeant. Cipolle picked it up and made to leave. "Not yet. Cipolle. Did I tell you to leave?"

The Sergeant frowned and shook his head while thinking, yes, you did, before returning to his seat.

Izzo stayed silent for a long moment, staring into space. The Sergeant tried to think if he had ever seen his boss this angry. Everyone in the police station knew that Izzo's patience was legendary, legendary until he lost it, that is. Cipolle had seen him lose control of that patience before, but it had always been a quick rant and then back to business. The boss had been fuming since he got back from his long lunch, what, ten minutes before? At least ten minutes of anger was unheard of.

"Do you know what just happened to me?" the inspector finally demanded. Cipolle knew the question to be rhetorical, so just remained in his seat with his mouth shut.

"I saw the Alliss boy in Posillipo. He is registered as an under-chef at that seafood place, La Orchidea."

"I know the one, over-priced, where the rich and famous hang out. Front for the Cucciolo clan?"

"Yes, that's the one. I saw the English boy leave with one of the clan soldiers. I was going to follow them, but a little old lady double parked and I couldn't get out. Can you believe that?" The last was an explosive shout that showed the mammoth effort the Inspector was making to keep a lid on his rage.

The Sergeant shook his head in sympathy, but he did believe it. It was probably the most common traffic violation in a city that boasted some of the worst drivers in the world. To a Neapolitan, the highway code was a book that you could use as toilet paper when your supply of Kleenex was inadvertently cut short. Few of the local drivers had ever read it, including the two men sitting in the office having the conversation. Cipolle recalled only the week before when the boss had double parked and blocked him from leaving after his night shift. He had to go into the station and ask Izzo to move his car. He knew the boss to be overreacting, but he also knew that it was best to let the man's anger run its course. Confronting him when in a mood like this would see him transferred back to the Black Cats.

"See that?" Izzo asked, pointing at the slip of paper that had landed on the desk when he threw it at Cipolle. "That's the number of the Punto that blocked me. Little old lady with grey hair," Izzo held his bunched fingers on top of his head, indicating a bun, Cipolle surmised. "Claimed to be deaf."

"Claimed to be deaf how?"

"Pointed at her ears and shook her head. Didn't believe it though, not for one second."

The Sergeant nodded and just looked at the paper. "What the fuck are you waiting for, Sergeant? Get it checked out."

Cipolle snatched up the piece of paper and ran to do Izzo's bidding.

While the Sergeant checked the vehicle registration, the Inspector started on a fresh box of paperclips. He broke the first few clips because of the anger he was finding so difficult to suppress. His elation of the morning when the identity of the unknown man in the CCTV footage had been discovered, fled with each slap of the steering wheel and scream at the little old lady in the car beside him. He thought he had seen light at the end of the tunnel. In his mind's eye, the double homicide was resolved, the Alliss boy had returned to his rightful place and the armed police officer from the Metropolitan Police Service was gone from his territory satisfied with the assistance he had received from his Italian colleagues. That was now all dust and ashes.

Thinking of the English police officer caused Izzo to wonder what had happened to the blond giant. He had not seen him since the incident in the restaurant when he was unable to stomach the Inspector's favourite starter. Cipolle's team had tailed him briefly, but they reported that he just seemed to have no idea what he was doing and did nothing except loiter about the town with a bemused expression. Izzo guessed he had been waiting for Moses to arrive and was surprised that he missed him being brought into the station earlier that same day. The arresting officers had not used any guile when they brought Moses in for questioning. Had Thumper been at his usual post, he surely would have seen them bringing him in. Probably went for coffee, Izzo thought, with a smile.

The Sergeant returned to the office a short time later with a bemused expression, like he had discovered some forgotten secret concerning the Fiat Punto.

"Well?" the inspector asked.

"It is the car of Mama Cucciolo."

"I knew it!" the inspector shouted as he slapped his desk with a hand which was still sore from slapping the steering wheel in his car.

This time the slap was because Izzo was mad at himself for falling into such a trap. He had assumed that the Cuccioli would not be aware he was searching for the Alliss boy, but he should have realized they would have been looking for any signs of a police presence. He also should have known that the family's soldiers would know him on sight. They probably studied photographs of DIA officers in the same way that Cipolle studied photographs of Camorriste. He guessed that they had spotted him even before he ordered his lunch.

"It seems like we need to add Mama Cucciolo to our files too, Cipolle."

"Yes, sir." The Sergeant hesitated before continuing, "I thought the Camorra kept women and children out of it?"

"It used to be the case. I guess it changed when they shot that twelve-year-old boy because he witnessed one of their murders."

"Ah, yes," Cipolle nodded his understanding.

"I've been an arse, Sergeant." Izzo said. The Sergeant nodded, recognising that that was as close to an apology as his boss would ever come.

Chapter 13

Archie would never admit that he closed his eyes for the fleeting seconds before he heard the gunshot. He would rather have said that he faced death with resilience and acceptance of the inevitable, but he had not. When the olive-skinned man in the Armani suit and Ray-Ban shades grinned, and shrugged, he knew it was over. He thought briefly of the futility of dying when simply looking for a missing person, and laughed inside at the irony of it. And then he heard the shot. Had it been over, he would not have heard the shot. The gun had been pointing between his eyes when he closed them and the bullet would have mashed his brains nanoseconds before his ears would register any sound.

He remained with his eyes firmly closed for a few seconds and took a deep breath. He could smell that cordite scent that pervades any shooting, but could feel no blood or pain. It was not possible that the Dago had missed from that range, surely? He opened his eyes. He could see the Alliss boy and the driver of the car helping the would-be shooter as they ran back through the arch the way they had come in. The teenage would be murderer was clutching his shoulder and his gun was lying under the arch where he had dropped it.

Archie looked over his shoulder and saw the tall blond-haired copper who he had clobbered in Roper's, standing at the opposite end of the short tunnel into the amphitheatre with a smoking pistol. Archie bent down and grabbed the discarded gun, expecting the copper to start shooting at him before he got up again. But there were no shots. The police officer just stood under the arch and watched him retrieve the weapon. Archie put the safety on and stuck the gun in the waistband of his trousers before walking over to the man, who did not move other than to put his own gun into a shoulder holster under his left arm.

The police officer was shaking slightly.

"First time I ever shot a man," he explained as Archie approached. Archie nodded and affected a knowing air, although he had never shot anything other than a wooden target on a firing range.

"We had better get out of here. That shot would have been heard back in Pozzuoli." The blond giant said.

"Better get your spent cartridge first." Archie wondered where that came from. How had he known to retrieve the cartridge? The man scuffed around in the dust with his foot for a few seconds before uncovering the cartridge.

"Shall we get out of here now?" he asked as he retrieved it.

Archie agreed and followed him out of the short tunnel and then out of the ruins, where he should have died. Neither of the men spoke as they walked, but they did keep their eyes open for any possible danger. There appeared to be none. The three men had disappeared.

"I have my car here," Thumper said as they left through the main exit. "I guess you also have transport." Archie nodded.

"Look, I think we need to talk."

"Yes, I think we do," Archie agreed.

"You can follow me. I have been keeping a low profile away from Pozzuoli and I guess we would be better not returning there today."

"Sounds good." Thumper noticed that Moses's responses were monosyllabic. It was obvious that the bodyguard was angry. The DS could not blame him, not really. He probably thought he had seen the last of The Met when he thumbed his nose at Thumper on the M4. It must have been something of an eye-opener to find the same police officer in the ruins of Pompeii.

Half an hour later they were sitting over grappas under the awning of a small bar in Castellammare di Stabia, south of Pompeii. It was early evening, so the locals were gathering and drinking their pre-dinner drinks. A few nodded in recognition of the Sergeant, but none spoke.

"What I don't get," Archie said, "Was how you came to be in Pompeii."

"I've been watching the station in Pozzuoli. I saw you arrive this morning and then waited for you to leave. I followed you there."

"What, in the Fiat?"

"Yeah, in the Fiat."

Archie frowned. He was obviously not as good at this game as he had been beginning to think. There seemed to have been a tandem of followers, and no one being followed had the slightest idea about it, until it all came crashing down in the tunnel, the arena where so many gladiators had given away their lives. But worse than that, one of the followers had been in a pink Fiat 500. Archie supposed he should be grateful though, because the copper had saved his life.

"Thanks, Bunny," he said, genuinely meaning it. If not for this bumbling giant of a man, Archie would have died in the dust under the arch. Thumper blushed and nodded.

"Why Bunny?" Archie felt the need to ask. The name had been on his mind since he had heard it in the nightclub. It seemed to be an incongruous name for a police officer.

"I'm DS Thumper, from SO14, hence Bunny." Archie shrugged, failing to see the connection. "Thumper was the rabbit in Bambi."

"Ah, gotcha," Archie said. "Wait a minute, isn't SO14 responsible for Royal Family and visiting dignitary security?"

"Yeah, I am one of HRH's personal protection detail." The DS said with some pride.

"So, what the hell are you doing chasing me all over Europe?"

"Orders."

"Orders?"

"Yes, I have been ordered to investigate you."

"What, SO14 performs investigations?"

"No, not really. We are a protection detail, but because I am incapacitated," he pointed at his knee. "Top Brass decided that I should do it, rather than hand it over to CID."

"Investigate me for what? Apart from defending my client, I haven't done anything."

Thumper shrugged. "Look I'm sorry, but orders is orders." Archie was a little of a military historian and he knew what had happened during the post-war trials in Nuremburg when the Nazis had tried to claim the same thing.

He scoffed, "Whose orders were they, anyway?"

"Came from the top, but it was my Super who ordered me. Said I was to throw the book at you."

Archie was beginning to lose his cool, just a little. "I don't get it, why didn't you just change your statement and charge me with assault?"

"There was no way the Brass would allow it. Too much of an embarrassment for them. As soon as your lawyer arrived, we informed him that we would not be pressing charges and you were free to go."

"Are you telling me that the bastard knew before he came into the interview room that I was free to go?"

"Yes."

"Fucker." Archie slammed his fist onto the table, which made the grappa glasses jump. He knew he should have just called Alliss from the phones out the front of Pompeii. He would be on his way home now, had he done so.

"I was angry when they told me they weren't pressing charges," the Sergeant explained. "I'm just as much in the dark as you are."

"Okay, I still don't get why you followed me here," Archie said.

"I didn't follow you. I got here before you."

"Yeah, how the hell did you manage that, anyway?" Archie had assumed that the blond giant was a bit thick, but he had to admit to himself that arriving in Pozzuoli before him illustrated a certain level of guile.

"The girl from the pub in Gloucester, forgot about a postcard from Alliss. He posted it in Pozzuoli. We guessed you'd get here eventually and so decided to get a leg up."

"Get a leg up? What the hell're you talking about?" Archie was thinking aloud as much as anything. As far as he knew, there was nothing to get a leg up on, or at least there had not been anything to get a leg up on. Archie supposed there might be now, now someone had just tried to kill him. He was bemused about what Thumper's bosses had hoped to achieve. What the hell did they think was going on? He was looking for a missing person, or at least that was what he thought he had been doing. Now he was not so sure. He wondered if this Sergeant's Brass knew more than they were letting on.

"How did you find out about Gloucester? I left you for dead on the M4."

"A black and gold Maserati is distinctive enough. I know some guys in traffic and they owed me one. You were tracked on CCTV right into Gloucester city centre. Finding you at the Cock 'n

Bull was pure luck. I needed a pint and pulled in just as you were leaving."

"Yeah, I saw you." Archie smiled his understanding and took a sip of his grappa to gather his thoughts.

"Have you got any idea what is going on?" Thumper asked.

"No, none. Listen, didn't you guys talk to the lawyer? He could have told you what was going on."

"No, after your release we just followed you. The Brass thought we'd hit the jackpot as soon as we knew you were after his son."

"What possible motive could I have for going after Alliss's son?"

"You're here aren't you. What else would you be doing here?"

"Philip Alliss asked me to track the boy down. I'm not *after* him. I'm tracking a missing person. There is a difference."

Thumper just shrugged. He did not profess to have any clue about the workings of the Top Brass's minds and why they thought Archie was up to no good. He did not think it pertinent to the current situation to admit that he too thought Archie was up to no good, or he used to think that. He had sort of admitted it to himself now that the Super was on some sort of crusade and that the investigation into Moses was highly irregular, if not actually illegal.

"I assume that one of the guys under the arch was Alliss?" he asked.

"Yeah, the white one."

"Why did the other guy try to shoot you?"

"Not sure, but judging by the look on his face, I'd say he tried to shoot me because he had a gun. My guess is he would have enjoyed pulling the trigger, regardless. He's a psycho."

Uttering that truth caused Archie to shake uncontrollably. It was as if the adrenalin that had kept him calm had worn off; as if admitting that he had almost died at the hands of a psycho with a big gun made it all real. He felt like vomiting.

"Here, you should have my grappa."

Archie nodded his appreciation of the gesture and quaffed the fiery liquid in one pull. To give Archie time to regain his composure, Bunny went to the bar and ordered a couple more. When he got back he put the drinks on the table and stuck out his hand, "I'm Dick Thumper. How about a truce?" Archie looked at the proffered hand briefly before succumbing and shaking it.

"Archie Moses."

"What now?" Thumper asked as he returned to his seat.

"Now we have to talk to Alliss Senior and find out what the fuck is going on."

They decided over several grappas that Thumper would fly to London. There were two reasons for the decision: he would bring more authority to bear on the lawyer and unlike Moses, he was not afraid of flying. The DS had watched the pain on Archie's face as he admitted his phobia. When he told the story of being unable to jump from the back of a Hercules and being ridiculed by his peers, Thumper felt a little pang of affection for him. The ugly bald git tried to come across as a gruff hard man, but there was a sensitive side, perhaps a more humane side.

An abject fear of flying was not something Archie carried lightly. He had shown a lot of reticence before finally admitting that he could not fly because of a fear of heights. Thumper showed his own sensitive side by nodding and not belabouring the point, as he might have been tempted to do. They knew that there was an element of urgency and driving was not an option. It was also agreed that getting a direct flight from Rome would be quicker. Thumper could get an early morning flight out and be back the same evening.

"I don't have the money for a ticket," the police officer admitted during the discussion, but Archie said he would buy a return ticket on his credit card, and that was the end of it. Decision made.

Chapter 14

He liked the Chicago White Sox. It was not one of the most well-known baseball teams on this side of the Atlantic, but that was one of the reasons he was attracted to it. He did not want to be one of the sheep and wear a cap that everyone else in the area was wearing; USS Nimitz, for example, or one of those stupid arse beer hats with straws through which you could drink Bud from a plastic cup on top of your head. Who cared that the Nimitz had been in the harbour only a few years before, dwarfing the other vessels and even making the backdrop of the city itself seem small? He certainly did not, although, he liked the Nimitz. And on top of that, he was not a beer drinker. If he had been a beer drinker, it would have been Bud for sure, but he preferred wine of the local variety, which was not poisoned with artificial ingredients. On a hot day, he would take it with soda water, what the Americans called a Spritzer. Yeah, he liked a White Wine Spritzer with loads of ice.

It was not only the Chicago White Sox and Spritzers he liked. He liked all things American. His sunglasses were Ray-Ban, his jocks were Calvin Klein, his lighter was a Zippo and his weapon of choice was a Smith & Wesson SW1911, not that he had it with him in the airport. No, when he got to London one of the family would provide him with a weapon. Besides, he did not think that he would need one, not really. It should be a straightforward in and out knife job and he could pick up a knife in any hardware store. He was glad, because he liked knife jobs best. Shootings were so impersonal, so matter of fact and over too quickly.

What he did not like were unforeseen complications. They had planned meticulously. They thought that they had covered all possible contingencies. They were wrong. The arrival of two unwelcome guests into the equation were, well, unforeseen and causing massive complications. For one of the brothers to have to travel to London was at the least an inconvenience. It meant that some of the critical stages of the operation would have to be handled solo, and in this instance by his brother. He trusted his brother and so felt it would remain just that, an inconvenience. He hoped it would be nothing more than an inconvenience, because if it turned into something more the boss would blame him, as he was the eldest. The boss did not take kindly to failure and the punishments she meted out were draconian.

They had been deciding on how best to handle the intrusion, when his cousin from the airline called with information about the police officer travelling to London. It presented a solution to their problems, but one of them had to go to London. They decided he would go because his brother needed a little time to recover from his shoulder injury, and might even be recognized, although the light under the arch had been poor. The wound was only a scratch, so would not impact on the overall operation; he could continue the further stages of the plan on his own. That did not lessen the annoyance of his being shot by a dumb English blond giant with a gun. None of the three had seen the man until after the shooting. His presence and that of the ugly Englishmen had been a surprise to all three.

After the shooting, they had asked their source in London for information about the man who had interrupted them under the arch and the blond giant who shot his brother. When the report about the Detective Sergeant and his quarry Moses arrived, the brothers had been both surprised and angry at the vagaries of fate. It was a pure coincidence that the two men had arrived on the scene when they did, but that arrival was causing the boy to wonder about what he was doing in Pozzuoli.

The presence of Chris Alliss was essential to the success of the ongoing plot, and having him waver through squeamishness at this late stage was at the least, very inconvenient. Mama said that the shooting in Pompeii made the boy want to go back to his father. That could not be allowed to happen and so this new phase had been introduced, which should rid them of the police officer and harden the boy's resolve. They thought that with the police officer out of the way, they could handle the other one easy enough.

He looked up from the Hello magazine he was pretending to peruse when the ground crew announced the imminent boarding of the flight to Luton. With a sigh, he left his seat and strolled to the departure gate queue, making sure that the blond man was in front of him. The tall English policeman had been late and he had started to worry that his cousin was wrong. It would be very upsetting if this unscheduled trip to London was for nothing.

Thumper hated that self-righteous "Bing-Bong" yet another flight has arrived on time. It was as if the airline expected a medal because they had provided a service for which the customer had paid. He also knew that they added at least a twenty-minute buffer to the regulation flying time so that the "Bing-Bong" would almost always be heard.

The flight had been more or less uneventful, but being a charter, the leg room for a man of Thumper's length was extremely tight. His seat area made the Fiat seem spacious. When he finally unfolded himself, and passed through the arrivals hall, he saw a bank of phones and decided to give Layla a call. It proved to be a wasted five minutes. The conversation consisted of only a few sentences before he slammed the receiver down and cursed. Why the hell did it always come down to what was best for Layla? He was risking his life for Queen and country, well for Christopher Alliss anyway, and all she could do was worry about the Fiat. He decided to concentrate on going to talk to Alliss Senior and getting to the crux of what exactly was going on.

There was no direct rail connection from Luton Airport to London City Centre, so the DS had to get a bus into the railway station and then a train into Kings Cross. He took the underground to Fleet Street where the offices of Alliss, Toft & Watts were located. Fleet Street was a short Tube ride from Kings Cross, and it was only a few minutes later when the DS was showing his warrant card to the attractive woman behind the reception desk and wondering if he would have time for a bag of fish and chips and a pint before he headed back to Pozzuoli.

"I need to see Philip Alliss."

"I am sorry Sergeant, Mr Alliss is not here today."

"It's urgent that I talk with him. It is about his son Christopher." Thumper used what he hoped was a grave expression, and tried to affect a pose that indicated he was legitimate, or pukka as he thought of it. "Do you know how I can contact him?"

"Well, as far as I know he is at home."

"Can you give me his home address?"

"I am not supposed to provide that sort of information." Thumper could see her internal conflict with the company rules and what she probably saw as an official request from a Metropolitan Police Officer. That indecision vindicated their choice of traveller, because if it had been Archie standing there in his fancy suit and his bald head, she would have adamantly refused to help. He smiled what he hoped was a winning smile, however inappropriate, and she relented.

"He has an apartment in West Kensington, I will get the address card out for you to copy."

"Are you doing anything later?" she asked as Thumper wrote the details from the address card into his flip pad. He smiled and nodded before waving goodbye and heading for the lifts.

Alliss's apartment was just another short Tube ride from Fleet Street, so Thumper was ringing the apartment intercom within half an hour of leaving the law firm offices. He was relieved when a metallic voice said, "Alliss. Who is it, please?"

"Good evening, sir, I am DS Thumper from The Met." Thumper decided to leave out what section of the police service he was with, but it proved futile.

"Aren't you the SO14 detective that my client incapacitated?"

"Yes sir, but..." Alliss did not allow him to continue.

"I cannot talk to you, Sergeant, it is a conflict of interest."

"Please, Mr Alliss, I know where your son is." There was a heavy pause then. The DS was about to give up and try to think of another approach, when the intercom buzzed and the door lock clicked. It was with relief that Thumper pushed open the door and called the lift.

Despite the receptionist's reticence about giving out the address of one of her bosses, and Alliss's own reticence about a conflict of interests, once the introductions and formalities were over and it was clear why he had arrived, Philip Alliss was glad that he had.

"So, you have seen Christopher?"

"Not me, Mr Alliss, it was Archie, I mean Moses who saw him. He was in the ruins of Pompeii with some dodgy Italian characters."

"Dodgy how, Sergeant? Rather, how do you know they were dodgy?"

"One of them was gonna take a pot shot at Archie, only I shot him first."

"So, you are wanted by the Italian police?"

"Not as far as I know. The man was a good thirty feet away, so I only winged him. He ran." Thumper left out that he had asked his friend Adam Standing to keep an eye open for Interpol notices, and so far, there were none. "Reckon he wouldn't have reported it."

"What makes you sure he would not have reported it?"

"I guess he would've had to report it if the wound had been serious enough to warrant a hospital visit, where he would have been reported to the police. Gunshot wound and all that. But like I said, I only winged him, so I reckon he wouldn't bother."

"I see. So why are you here, DS Thumper?"

"Well, sir, I chased Archie to Pozzuoli in Italy near Naples. Sort of chased him anyway."

"What do you mean sort of, Sergeant?"

"I got a heads-up and so arrived before him. After the events in Pompeii, we teamed up…"

Alliss interrupted, "I am really not sure why you were chasing my client in the first-place?"

"Sorry, sir. Let me go back to the beginning," which he duly did, explaining events from when Dugs had given him the ridiculous assignment, to when he shook Archie's hand over grappas.

"So, you see, Mr Alliss, we need to get a handle on what is happening. There's no way that Archie is gonna allow someone threaten his life and not do something about it."

Philip Alliss raised his eyebrows and nodded his understanding. He could well believe that Archibald Moses would hold a grudge. He did not understand why the two of them had paired up, or why Moses was still in Italy. After all, he had fulfilled his obligation to Alliss, but if only for the sake of Christopher, he was willing to provide the DS with everything that he knew.

"Hold that thought Sergeant. I will put the kettle on and make us some tea. Then we can discuss what I suspect is going on."

Moses saw Thumper exit from the arrivals gate in Fiumicino and wandered over to the barrier. He could see that the Sergeant was in pain with his leg, the limp was more pronounced than when he had left the day before.

"So, how did it go?" he asked.

"I dunno, did you ever get the feeling that it's all out of your control, you know like when you end up carrying dog crap all around the park?"

It was obvious from his expression that Archie did not understand the reference to dog crap, "Why would you be carrying dog crap anywhere?"

"You know it's the law, if your dog takes a dump, you have to pick it up."

"Are you telling me that when your dog has a shite you pick it up?"

"Of course, it's the law."

"I don't think I've ever seen anyone pick up dog shit before."

"Most people don't bother."

"So, why do you?"

"I'm a police officer, if I don't uphold the law, who will?"

"Who enforces it, anyway?"

"Dunno, never really thought about it."

Archie laughed. Thumper was going to take umbrage, but when he looked over at his new partner, he could see there was no malice in the laugh, so he laughed, too.

"So, what do you mean exactly, you feel like you're carrying dog crap everywhere?"

Thumper hesitated because he had lost his train of thought, but eventually continued, "When you take your dog for a walk in the park, you can guarantee that he won't take a dump until after you pass a bin and it's so far back it's not worth returning, so you have to walk around the park with it wrapped in newspaper until you arrive at the exit where the next bin is. That's how I feel this investigation is going. It's like we just passed a bin and now we are carrying shit around with nowhere to put it."

"Murphy's law, you mean?" Archie asked.

"Yeah, sort of, I suppose. You had much activity round 'ere?"

Moses shook his head. "I've been keeping tabs on the dapper copper, but he seems to have reached a dead end. At least he ain't been up to much while you were away."

"Okay, let's exchange notes on the drive down to Pozzuoli."

About forty-five minutes later Moses and Thumper were driving down the A1 motorway heading for Naples. The traffic was so intense that Moses had to concentrate on the road a good deal more than usual, but he still needed to know what had happened in London.

"So, what did he say?" Archie asked.

"It seems the boy is trying to get back at his father because the lawyer had not been there when the mother died. Usual family stuff."

"Why wasn't he there? Divorce?"

"No, it seems that in later life Alliss Senior discovered he was gay and moved out." Archie nodded his understanding. Of course, the boy felt betrayed and abandoned.

"They never divorced, but he transferred the family home into this wife's name and bought a pad in West Kensington."

"How's the boy trying to get back at him, exactly?"

"Sold the mother's house. Calls in the middle of the night and then refuses to talk. Sends shitty post cards. You know, the usual family shite." If that was usual, Archie felt glad that he was an orphan.

"Apparently, the lawyer got a postcard last week to say that Alliss Junior was working in a restaurant owned by the old family back home. By the way, Alliss is not the lawyer's real name, not his original name, anyway. He is of Neapolitan descent. Seems his name used to be Filippo Elenco, and he changed it before he went to uni in the UK."

"So what? I'm sure he ain't the first Italian who changed his name."

"No, but apparently, his father was an accountant and he worked for some family called Cucciolo before leaving Naples for Luton. That family has a reason to be upset, too."

"Really?"

"Yeah, it seems that the father helped himself to some funds, bit of a leg up for himself and his family when they arrived in Luton."

"So, grandad robbed the clan and legged it to Luton? Why Luton of all places?"

"That's where the charters that fly from Southern Italy always land. There is a huge Italian population in Luton and Dunstable. It's a bit like when they get off a bus, they mill about and set up roots in the same place where they first hit the pavement, like the cement's still wet, or summat."

"So the boy contacted his ancestors and that has kicked up a shit storm?"

"Yeah, they had no idea where Alliss was until now. Don't ask me how the boy got in touch with the old family, or even knew of their existence, the lawyer has no idea."

"Alliss Junior must have had some idea of his father's origins, surely?"

"Alliss Senior says not. He guessed they came from Italy, because of grandad's accent, but was never given any details."

"So somehow, we will probably never know how, he gets wind of this Mafia family in Pozzuoli and they send him an invite to "come on down". Hence the postcard in Eindhoven."

"Yep, that's my guess."

"And now this Cucciolo family want revenge."

"Yeah, even though the old man is dead years, Alliss Senior thinks they want payback."

"So, the kid's in trouble."

"Philip Alliss certainly thinks so. He's glad that they haven't come after him, but thinks it is because they intend to punish him through Christopher."

"He hasn't had any indication that he's being watched or anything?"

"No, nothing. He thinks they are concentrating on the boy for now. Thinks they are setting him up to get back at his father and grandfather. Philip reckons that while the boy's okay, he will be, too."

"I bet he wants us to intervene?"

"Yeah, he asked if I thought we could get his son out. I said that I thought we could." Thumper looked questioningly at Archie. Archie nodded.

"As soon as we get the kid out, he's gonna seek police protection."

"So, what exactly are we going to do?"

"I know this is going to sound way off base, but I think we should go to Izzo with what we've got."

"I was starting to think the same thing. He told me from the get go that he is Mafia police. I reckon he should know what to do."

Chapter 15

Philip Alliss was sitting at his kitchen table reading a report on Archibald Moses, which an old university friend had sent over from MoD archives the day that Moses was arrested. After the visit from DS Thumper, he wanted to get a feel for the two men who were going to try and save his son from a fate he would rather not contemplate.

Thumper had seemed completely guileless during their chat earlier that afternoon, and Alliss had no doubts about how the DS would deal with the adversity of any situations that might arise. He was a plodding hulk of a man who would doggedly continue with something until he reached the result he wanted, or died trying. Alliss was reading the report because he wanted to get a sense of whether Moses would do the same.

The talk with the Sergeant over tea that afternoon had made Alliss aware of just how upset he felt by his son's betrayal. Chris had been acting like a spoilt dick ever since Philip came out and left him and his mother, but for him to seek retribution on this scale? It scared Philip. However, when all was considered, he was still the boy's father and he still loved him with a passion.

Alliss turned his attention to the document. It was quite detailed, but did not provide anywhere near a complete picture.

He had to read between the lines to get a true sense of the Moses character. He could tell that as a youngster, the bodyguard had had a hard life. He read how Archie was abandoned by his mother, and how he had been nameless when he was discovered by the Mother Superior at the Sisters of Mercy orphanage in Ealing, wrapped in swaddling and deposited in a wicker basket.

Had the report been more detailed, he would have read how Mother Agnes had answered the door, thrown back the covers to see what gift had been left for the sisters, blanched and taken a step back. The report would not have reported however, how 'Jesus Christ, what an ugly fucker', had fled through her mind as she looked. Nor how many a 'hail Mary' had later been given in atonement.

Alliss supposed that a woman's normal reaction on discovering a helpless child in need of nurturing would be to revert to her natural mothering instincts, but he surmised from the report that on that morning, Mother Agnes's only instinct was to call the police and report the abandonment.

It was obvious to Alliss that the police came and immediately called social services. And when social services came they had no one else to call and so took the baby away. Alliss surmised that they returned the unnamed boy within a week and that Mother Agnes never heard from either the police or social services again, at least not in relation to the baby's parentage.

The lawyer was not wrong in his assumptions.

When the nuns registered the boy shortly after he was returned, they named him Archibald because that had been the name of Mother Agnes's father, and unfortunately for the boy, Moses because he had been found in a wicker basket.

Archie then grew up in a hostile environment. It was not just because of the nun's poor choice of moniker. Archie had been an ugly boy and that, coupled with the type of institute in which he was raised, meant a life of abject misery. Over time, the nuns accepted the boy for who he was and not what he was, but that was not true of his peers.

As Archie grew, his hair failed to grow with him, because his string of luck continued with a dose of alopecia universalis. Not only was he ugly, he was also bald, which became an issue from quite an early stage in his pre-pubescence. Kids are cruel. Kids in an orphanage can be far more than cruel. Kids in the Sisters of Mercy orphanage were no different, and it was only a matter of time before Archibald became Bald Archie.

Kids often channel their energies at one target. Especially if that target is different from them and vulnerable, as it was in Archie's formative years and early puberty. However, unfortunately for the other kids in the institution, Archie was not only extremely ugly and hairless, he was also extremely strong. It did not take long into his puberty for him to discover his strength and when he did, there was no holding him back from revenge. Anyone who attempted to make him the target of any bullying from that moment, regretted their decision. There was a short spate of quite serious, if not life-threatening injuries, for which the culprit was never discovered, before the bullying of Archie stopped for good.

Because he had been the butt of group bullying for more than a decade by his peers and little had been done by the sisters in the orphanage to prevent it, he wanted payback. Unlike the other orphans, Archie was not only cunning and strong but also extremely intelligent. Things began to happen: thefts occurred, wanton damage occurred, more non-attributable injuries occurred. Again, no culprit was ever immediately obvious. The victims pretended to suspect each other, despite understanding who the culprit was. The nuns suspected all of the children, although secretly hoping it was Archie. The atmosphere in the orphanage became tense and even more unpleasant than is usual in that type of institution. Archie enjoyed himself enormously until he was eventually caught by a fortuitous coincidence of the type that has resulted in many being apprehended who would have otherwise escaped notice.

For his most daring escapade in the string, Archie used a ladder to climb into the Mother Superior's cell through an open window and leave an unpleasant surprise in her cot. The caretaker, while doing his outside chores saw the ladder propped against the wall and removed it because he was prone to memory lapses and thought he must have left it earlier. It was anyone's guess what the caretaker thought he might have been doing with a ladder propped against the window of Mother Superior's cell, but that was a different issue. As it happened, the cells were as hard to get out of without a key as they were to get into without a key and so Archie had no means of escape. He was discovered by Mother Agnes when she retired for the night. Not only was he in her cell at sundown, but he had left a nicely formed turd in the middle of her pillow, which was augmented by a week of cabbage-based diet and so stank to "high heaven". He could provide no vindication for his presence in the cell with a very ripe shite, and so his spate of vandalism was discovered. Mother Agnes put two and two together and made fifty-six all in the blink of an eye. Anyone who could conceive of such a vindictive plot could conceive of anything, surely. So, she decided Archie was the perpetrator of all the recent wrongdoing.

As she had when Archie first appeared, the Mother Superior immediately called the police. When the wooden tops arrived, and despite there being a lack of evidence to support any such theory, Mother Agnes laid at Archie's feet every malfeasance that had occurred in the orphanage since he had been old enough to walk. She never wanted the boy and saw the current situation as being ideal to remedy that problem. The cops took a shine to Archie, and not in a positive way. They told the Mother Superior that he should join the army cadets before he either killed someone or became a permanent resident of Wormwood Scrubs through repeated criminal offences. The Chief Super of the Metropolitan Police Service Ealing, over on the Uxbridge Road, was a member of the same golf club as the CO of the Aldershot Army Cadets, and so many an adolescent reprobate ended up in the Cadets at the behest of the Ealing police force, it being a standing order of the Chief Super.

Mother Agnes failed to see the irony of preventing the boy from killing by sending him to an institution whose sole purpose was to instil discipline in youngsters so they would be better able to kill, and gave him over to military life.

"Is that you, Chris?" Philip called in hope. He had heard a noise out in the hall that sounded like a stealthy foot fall. When there was no answer, he sighed, turned the report over and went out into the hall.

Alliss stared at the man wearing the Chicago White Sox baseball cap. The cap was black and had a gothic script 'Sox' angled in white that gave it a sinister look. He had no real idea how he came to be looking at this man while tied to a chair in his own kitchen. He had walked out into the hall to investigate the noise and was now waking up with no recollection of what had happened. The back of his head was throbbing though, so he assumed someone had been waiting in the hall and had clobbered him when he walked out of the kitchen.

He was naked. His arms were tied behind the chair where he had been sitting when reading the MoD report on Moses. The man in the cap had not seen Alliss regain consciousness, because he was perusing the report, punctuating his reading with the occasional tut, or a smile. Alliss tried not to move and let the man know that he had come to his senses. Somehow, he knew that as soon as the man saw that he was awake, his day would take a decided downturn.

His legs were aching, as if he had been standing on the balls of his feet for several minutes and the circulation had been cut off. His calves were tied to the chair legs and he squirmed involuntarily to try and loosen the bonds slightly, which caused the man in the cap to look up and see that he was awake.

"Hello, you're up," he said with a friendly 'no need to be worried smile'. Philip knew that the smile was a lie. Despite the peak of the cap, he could see that the man's eyes were cold, almost lifeless. There was a stench of evil about their owner, with his Armani suit and patent leather bespoke shoes. Not that Philip had ever encountered real evil, but his capacity to intuit a danger was heightened during his early days as a homosexual. Homophobia was still ripe in the city, despite it being the end of the twentieth century, and homophobic beatings were commonplace. It became a necessity to recognize the homophobes and change to the other side of the road, or turn around and head in the opposite direction. It was that sixth sense which warned him of the imminent danger. He could see the tone of his assailant's skin as well and there was a definite oliveness about it.

So, they have *not* forgotten me, he thought, I should have known better, with an inward smile.

The man pulled up a breakfast stool and sat looking down at Philip with his hands on his thighs. "I am guessing that you are Philip Alliss. Just nod if you are." He nodded.

"He seems like a bit of a loose cannon, this man Moses," the man said, nodding in the direction of the report. "He has caused all sorts of difficulty with your son, Christopher."

Alliss tried to ask about Chris, but something was lodged firmly in his mouth, so all he could manage was a grunt. He hoped that the look he was giving the man was speaking volumes on his behalf.

The man looked at him and laughed. "What is it, you English say? 'If looks could kill'. Yes, if looks could kill I would be dead, and your life would be so much easier. I am going to ask you a few questions. If you answer them, you will not be harmed. Do you understand?"

The man spoke with an American accent, but there was a hint of something else, as if he had spent time in The States but did not come from there. Philip did not really need clues as to where the man originated. He knew he came from Southern Italy as surely as he knew his time on this earth was heavily restricted. The Latino put a hand to the side of his face and leaned his head over slightly with a smile that showed the whitest teeth Philip Alliss had ever seen. He caught himself wondering how he had managed to get them so white and then wondered at the capacity of the human mind to divert onto the most mundane of things in times of extreme stress.

"Do you know what? When I said I was going to ask you a few questions, I lied. You don't have any information I want. I have you trussed up like a Thanksgiving turkey because I love inflicting pain."

Philip tried to shout "No!", but the gag, whatever it was, meant the word came out as a muffled scream.

Chapter 16

"Bond." The AC answered his mobile phone tersely. He always answered it tersely without really understanding why. He supposed it might be because he never really got used to any of the new technologies and it always surprised him when it rang. That and because he preferred Margery to filter out those callers he would rather not speak to. Not many people had the AC's mobile number and they knew to ring it only in an emergency, so despite hating to do so, he always answered.

"Good evening, sir, Commander Blythe."

"Why didn't you ring the office number, Commander? I am still at my desk."

"I thought I ought to call you directly, sir." Bond frowned then. His senior executives only called his mobile when they were worried that the information they wanted to convey might be leaked out of the confines of their inner circle. The mobile phones of each officer in The Met were not standard. Their signals were encrypted and could not be listened to by members of the public.

"I am at a murder scene, sir, over in West Kensington. I think you need to get over here."

"Where exactly is here, Commander?" He could hear the Commander repeating the question to whoever was in earshot and knew the address. Derek Blythe was fond of his driver privilege and preferred to be driven everywhere, so never really knew where he was other than vaguely. The Assistant Commissioner was known to get quite upset about the affected nature of some of his senior officers, feeling that they should concentrate more on the job than the benefits it carried.

He wrote down the address and pressed the intercom. "Margery, have my car meet me out front in five minutes, would you."

Twenty minutes later, Assistant Commissioner Bond was sitting on a breakfast stool next to Detective Sergeant Standing in the crowded kitchen of an apartment in West Kensington. Scene of Crime Officers (SOCOs) were dusting for prints and taking photographs. The naked remains of an IC one male, assumed to be Philip Alliss, were tied to a kitchen chair both by the arms and the legs. His sightless eyes were staring at the floor between his knees. His chin was hanging near his chest because his throat had been cut from ear-to-ear. Bond could see what appeared to be a black tea-towel hanging from the victim's mouth, probably a gag. Deep cigarette burns, multiple bruises and shallow knife cuts on his upper thighs, chest and arms indicated that he had been severely tortured before he died.

The AC looked over at Standing. "Okay, Sergeant, it is my understanding that you rang this in?"

"Yes, sir."

"Let's have it, then." DS Standing nodded and looked at his notepad, more for reassurance than because he could not recall the sequence of events.

"We had the apartment under surveillance from an unmarked van out the front of the block. There are spy cameras outside the front door of the residence, and the phone is tapped. These measures are in accordance with a directive from Commander Blythe." Standing looked up to make sure that the AC was following. Bond nodded for him to continue. "When plod arrived at the apartment door we came in to investigate."

"Plod, Sergeant?"

"Special Constables sir."

"Say what you mean, man!" Bond knew what detectives meant by Plod, but he felt that they should avoid the use of colloquialisms when speaking to senior officers. Strictly speaking, he felt they should avoid the use of colloquialisms and abbreviations, full stop, because he was an Orwellian when it came to the bastardization of the English language.

"Carry on, Sergeant," he sighed.

"The upstairs neighbours called in a disturbance sir, because of what sounded like muffled screaming. They couldn't say it was definitely screaming because of the radio."

"Radio?" Bond interrupted.

"Yes, sir. When we arrived at the apartment, the radio was so loud, we doubted that Mr Alliss could hear our knocking, so we broke the door in." Bond knew that breaking and entering was justified when there was probable cause.

"You found him like this, Sergeant? Already dead I mean."

"Yes, sir."

"Did you see anybody entering or leaving the apartment during your surveillance?" The Sergeant hesitated for several seconds before Bond prompted him, "Well man, did you?"

"Yes, sir."

"Were they known, Sergeant?"

"Yes, sir." Bond realized that the detective Sergeant was prevaricating and felt an unease at what the possible reasons could be. It was more than a Sergeant's job would be worth if he was discovered to be withholding information from his AC.

"Who, then, Sergeant, who?" Bond's patience wore ever thinner as Standing failed to say who had been seen entering and leaving the apartment. "Why the reticence man? Spit it out!"

DS Standing looked at commander Blythe for support, but Blythe just stood there with his arms crossed and a frown on his face.

"It was DS Thumper, sir!" Standing eventually blurted.

Bond raised an eyebrow and looked at commander Blythe. The name seemed familiar, but he could not place it. Commander Blythe shrugged his shoulders and glared at Standing, willing him to be more explicit. "DS Thumper, sir, the sarge that got 'is knee busted in Roper's the other night." Standing's enunciation took a nose dive with the pressure.

Assistant Commissioner Bond shivered as he realized the implications of what the Sergeant said. "You're sure, man?"

"The cast had gone, but it was 'im. 'Ee was limpin', like."
Standing did not really understand why he felt the need to
elaborate. He had known Dick Thumper for years and would have
recognised him anywhere.

"At what time was he seen entering and leaving the
building?"

"Around the time the neighbours thought the radio had first
been turned up, sir."

"Get everybody out, Commander." The AC said.

"You heard the man, out, all of you."

"When did this happen?" the AC asked Blythe, waving
around the room to indicate that he meant the murder.

"Forensics are ongoing sir, but the neighbours called to
complain about the muffled screaming, which might have been the
radio at ten past five. They said the radio was turned up between
three and four o'clock."

"Between three and four o'clock?"

"Yes, sir. There was some discrepancy between them. The
man says the radio was turned up at three, the woman says it
wasn't turned up until four."

Bond looked at his watch. It was now six in the evening. If
Thumper had been in the West Kensington apartment between
three and four and was intent on returning to the south of Italy
where he was supposed to be, he might be caught by an All Ports
Warning. "What do you think, Commander, an APW?"

The commander put his hand on his chin and thought before
responding. "It is worth a try, sir. He might not have left the country

yet and if he is still here, we surely need to talk to him to find out what is going on."

"Do it, then. And Blythe."

"Yes, sir?"

"Meet me in my office in one hour. We need to have a chat." The commander nodded before leaving the kitchen. AC Bond looked at Philip Alliss then, "What secrets are you keeping from me Mr Alliss?" he asked.

Margery poured two glasses of dry sherry and then left the office.

"Anything from the APW?" the AC asked Blythe.

"No, sir. Either we were too late, or he has not left the country."

"We have officers at his apartment?"

"Yes, sir. However, DS Thumper has not returned there either. I don't think he will be going to Peckham, sir."

"Would that not be unusual, Commander? I mean, not visiting his wife and kids."

"No, sir. Not judging by the way his wife is driving our constables up the walls."

"Ah, I see. What about Douglas or Willett, have they heard from him?"

"No, sir. There is nothing."

AC Bond took a sip of his sherry, gathering his thoughts before he said, "I want your considered opinion, Commander. Do you think that the DS has been turned in some way by the Mafia in Naples?"

Blythe guessed that this was the real reason why the AC had asked to see him in his office. He needed to know what the chances were that DS Thumper might have been bought by the Italian Mafia. Or if not bought, then perhaps threatened. That was the main reason why the officers in his Peckham apartment were SO19 and not SO7. They were there to protect the Sergeant's family as well as to apprehend him if he arrived there, although no one really expected the murder suspect to return to his flat. Granted, he was a bit thick, but he knew his street craft. He had to, to be such a good security officer.

Commander Blythe hesitated. He knew that the AC would take the overall blame if the Sergeant had indeed murdered the lawyer, for whatever reason. But Blythe had read the Sergeant's docket in his car on the way over. He did not know the man, and dockets were often misguided, but he could see nothing that would indicate DS Thumper could be turned, not even by a threat to his family. In fact, his career had been exemplary. He knew that the standing order regarding threats was to report them, and according to his file, Thumper followed orders to the letter. The CCTV footage and the fact that the Sergeant's prints were all over the apartment did not mean he was guilty of murder. Others had been seen entering and leaving the block. Any one of them might have killed the lawyer. There was also very little real security in the block or in the lawyer's apartment, so access through somewhere other than the front door could not be ruled out. Forensics had not discovered any evidence of a break-in, but that did not mean one had not happened.

The Commander took the plunge. "No, sir, I don't think so. I spoke to Dugs and he seems to think that Thumper is a good officer. I read his report, and if it is accurate, I would side with Dugs's assessment. No, I think there is another explanation."

The AC sighed, relief evident on his face. The last thing he needed now was a renegade. There was a chance, however small, that he would make it onto the New Year's honours list this year, and a blot of that magnitude would surely put paid to any chance of that happening.

"So, what about this murder? How does the DS fit into the equation?"

"We really need to talk to the Sergeant to answer that question, sir."

"Do we have any motive for the murder? Why would anybody torture and kill a respected city lawyer? What is it all about?"

"I don't know. Nothing was stolen. There is no sign of a break-in. I think we can only assume that it is in relation to his previous life as Filippo Elenco."

The AC nodded. "So, we now believe that…?"

"We know that the Alliss boy is somehow connected with a syndicated family out of the Naples region. We have the recorded GCHQ intercept that has him cited by name."

The AC nodded his understanding.

"We know that the father of Alliss emigrated to Luton in the late sixties and that Philip Alliss was already born and was with him. Our Italian cousins have told us that grandad Elenco was an accountant for a Mafia family in the region of Naples. We are guessing that when they emigrated it was under some sort of a cloud. Christopher Alliss, reaching out to his paisani, very likely tipped them off to his father's whereabouts."

"What do you think the torture is all about?"

"I would put it down to two possibilities, either the killer is a psychopath, or there is some message intended in the method of the victim's demise."

"Do you still think we need to sit on our hands and wait?" Bond asked.

"No, sir. I think things have come to a head. We need to act and act quickly."

"Yes, I was thinking the same. My feeling is to send in some support." Commander Blythe nodded his agreement and the ACSO picked up his mobile phone to make the call.

Chapter 17

Detective Sergeant Adam Standing had never been to the ACSO's office and he was a little nervous about having been called there now. If he was to make a guess, he would say that he was in trouble because of his reticence when being grilled by the Assistant Commissioner in the West Kensington apartment. He had been reluctant to tell the AC about Dick's visit to the apartment of Philip Alliss, because he knew that they would overreact and issue an APW. His reticence was immediately vindicated. As soon as he told the brass, they issued an All Ports Warning.

He might be alone in it, but DS Standing did not believe Dick had brutally murdered the lawyer. Admittedly, Dick was a bulk of a bloke, but those who knew him, knew he was as soft as putty. Adam and Dick had been friends for a long time. They had joined Specialist Operations together. Thumper ended up in SO14 because he did not have the killer instinct generally required for serious and organized crime investigations. Being an officer in SO7 needed undercover work, which only those of a hardened disposition like Standing would survive. Also, Dick had a wife and two very young boys at the time, which influenced the Specialist Operations selectors when they decided where to put him.

Now, late in the evening of the Alliss murder, Standing was sitting in a red leather armchair pretending to read Horse and Hound, which had been at the top of a pile of other magazines the DS would not dream of reading were he anywhere else. Not that he was reading Horse and Hound. He was just looking at the pictures. The ACSO's PA, Margery, kept giving him surreptitious glances, as if his presence was an affront to her sensibilities. He did not care if he was offending her sensibilities, though. His role in SO7 often had him offending people, because it was part of that function. The fact that he usually offended them with a punch to the face or a kick to the groin made him smile. Thinking about Margery bending over with a grunt of pain helped ease the tension.

His ears pricked up when the intercom on her desk buzzed and she flicked the switch to receive. "Yes, Commissioner," she said.

Standing pretended nonchalance and continued to flick through the pages of the magazine. From where he was sitting, the AC's voice sounded like the squawk of a large bird so he was unable to decipher what was said.

"He is ready for you now," Margery told him without looking in his direction. He smiled as he walked past her desk. I know you, he thought. She was no different from the masses who were oblivious to the role he and others like him played in the defence of the realm.

The DS knocked and walked into the office without waiting for permission. He was surprised to see his boss, Commander Blythe, also there.

"Good evening, DS Standing. I trust you managed to get finished in Kensington before I called," the AC said. Standing nodded. "The Commander is here in his capacity as leader of the serious and organized crime section, not because he is your governor."

The DS felt a little gratitude then. When he saw that the Commander was sitting in the red leather armchair, he was convinced he was in for a carpeting. Bond's brief sentence was probably intended to allay that fear and, if that were the case, it had worked.

"Yes, sir," he said.

"I think you know this man," the AC asked as he handed the DS a copy of the mugshot taken of Moses the night he was arrested.

Standing looked at the picture and frowned. "Yeah, Bald Archie Moses, not a bloke I am ever likely to forget." He had spent a couple of hours in an interview room with Moses the previous Friday night and never wanted the experience to be repeated.

"Can you tell me what you know about him, please, Sergeant."

"I interviewed him after he clobbered Dick Thumper in Roper's last week. He was an orphan, who had it tougher than most, seemingly. Then he joined the army. Apparently, he tried for the SAS but failed when he was unable to jump from a Herc."

"Do you know anything more about him?" Standing shook his head. He knew only what he had read before entering the interview room on that fateful Saturday morning, which was not much.

"Commander," the commissioner handed the reins over to his subordinate. Not only did Commander Blythe know more, Bond liked to assert his authority by delegating.

"You know that Sergeant Thumper is wanted in relation to the Alliss murder?" Standing nodded. "And that he was officially suspended from duty last week?" Again, Standing nodded.

Everyone at The Yard knew that Dick Thumper had been suspended for moonlighting in Roper's. They were all on edge, because they thought there would be an executive order banning them from their main source of income, but no such order had yet been handed down. The consensus was that Thumper would be charged with gross misconduct and booted out of the service.

"Unofficially, DS Thumper was investigating Archibald Moses. We cannot condone violence against this city's police service, otherwise anarchy will reign, but neither can we press charges against Moses, because public knowledge of the affair is not an option." Standing nodded.

"Well, we now have a situation in the south of Italy. DS Thumper followed Moses to a town near Naples called Pozzuoli." The Commander frowned at the spelling of the town. "I hope I'm pronouncing it correctly. We think that Alliss Senior was murdered because his son has become involved in something illicit in that area. It's important to stress that we are guessing, but we think that either Moses or Thumper, or both, have stumbled onto that illicit activity."

The DS frowned at his feet. He had not been asked to sit down, and although he was not getting a grilling from these two senior officers, it felt like he was. He was not buying into it either. It seemed obvious to him that they were not being entirely honest and he did not like it.

"With all due respect, sir, I was never one to take kindly to being led up the garden path."

"Of course, Detective. I fully intend to tell you everything that we know." The commander then proceeded to tell the DS about Alliss's history, why Moses was suspected of following the Alliss boy to Naples and why they thought Alliss Senior might have been murdered. He did not, however, mention the Red Brigade and their suspected involvement. The AC thought that the call that GCHQ intercepted was a little above the Detective's pay grade, but also the possible involvement of a defunct terrorist organization probably had little or no bearing on the operation.

"I see, sir," Standing said when the Commander had finished. "And exactly what do you want me to do?"

"We feel that we need to get hold of Thumper as soon as possible to get a handle on what is going on. It seems apparent that the easiest way for us to get in touch with him would be through this man Moses."

"How so, sir?" Standing interrupted.

Blythe frowned before answering. It seemed to him that the Detective was being impertinent. But then he remembered they were going to ask him to do an awful lot, so he relented. "DS Thumper was observed by your surveillance entering the apartment of Alliss before he was brutally murdered." Standing nodded.

"We suspect that Moses was hired by Alliss to track down his son, which led him to that town near Naples." The Commander seemed to be itemizing the points like a school teacher would with a challenged pupil. "Ergo, Thumper must be working with Moses."

That seemed to be quite a leap to the DS. There could have been any number of reasons why Thumper had visited the lawyer. It did not necessarily follow that the two of them were working together.

"We had an APW out on Thumper, but it was not quick enough to prevent him returning to Italy on an evening flight into Fiumicino airport in Rome. That flight landed over an hour ago, so we have lost him again. Both myself and the AC think that Thumper must be working with Moses, otherwise why visit Alliss Senior and then return to Italy, without even contacting his wife?"

The DS continued to frown at his feet. He believed that these two were still intent on getting Thumper for the murder of Alliss and needed some help. They knew that he was perhaps the best qualified man for the job and that he and Thumper were friends, so all was a ruse to get him to find Dick. He let it rest, though. If he could find Dick, he would do it, but for Dick's sake, not for the gratification of these two plonkers and the bureaucracy they represented.

Following the ACSO's instructions, Margery booked the Detective Sergeant a Monarch flight from Luton in the early hours of the following morning. She also booked him into the Luton Airport Hotel so there would be no issue with the early morning flight.

Standing was unmarried and without commitments, so he took a train to Luton and then a cab to the airport hotel as soon as he left The Yard. He decided to pick up the essentials for the trip in Luton airport after he was settled into the hotel room. A couple of hours later he had checked in and was heading for the lifts when he noticed a man sitting in the lobby, apparently reading a newspaper. He would have been innocuous except for the baseball cap. It was a black Chicago White Sox cap, which was not only not required in the lobby of a hotel, it was also totally out of place with everything else he wore. As he passed, the DS glanced at the man because the cap had caught his attention, and saw the deep olive shade of his skin. Standing knew that shade of skin tone was most common in the southern areas of Latin countries like Spain and Italy, and his professional instincts kicked in. The DS always paid attention when his sixth sense warned him of impending danger. Sometimes it could be wrong, but he had to react even when that was the case. If the hunch was right and he did nothing, he could end up dead.

Instead of getting a lift to the fifth floor, as he had originally intended, he ambled into the bar to the left of the hotel lobby. There was a column between the lobby and the bar door behind which he would briefly be out of the tail's sight. He walked into the bar and darted quickly to the right and stood with his back to the wall where he could see those who entered, but they could not see him.

The man came through the door only seconds after Standing reached the wall. The Latino was affecting a nonchalant pose with the newspaper under his arm, but the DS knew his eyes would be darting behind the Ray-Bans where they were hidden from view. Standing smiled when the man's head turned in his direction. He knew he had been spotted, but instead of panicking the man walked to the bar, sat down and ordered a white wine spritzer.

Standing did not move from where he was leaning against the wall. He could see the Latino and wondered about the man's dress sense, because a professional would go to great lengths to remain unnoticed. This man seemed to have the opposite agenda. But at the same time, an amateur would have panicked as soon as he realized he had been spotted. The Armani suited Latino simply waltzed up to the bar and ordered a white wine spritzer. Whatever else he was, Adam knew that this man was lethal. He was not easily fazed and he carried himself with a confidence that can only come from experience.

The DS stood up from the wall and waved at the Latino as he left to take a lift to his fifth-floor room.

During the rest of that evening, the DS caught several more glimpses of his unwanted shadow. He was in the hotel lobby when Standing went to the airport to buy toothpaste and underwear. He was in the bar when the DS went for a nightcap before turning in. The next morning, the Latino was in the restaurant eating the buffet breakfast. Standing thought he had lost him during the taxi ride to the airport, only to see him smiling benignly through the glass of the departure gate doors when he was heading through airport security. For some reason, the tail did not follow him into departures to see which plane he took. That he would be flying was obvious and it would have been easy enough to book a cheap charter so he could follow the DS to his departure gate. Standing waved again as he reached the end of the security queue and the man nodded at him with a grin.

During the flight, the DS studied the dockets the AC had provided him with the previous day. He knew Dick Thumper well, but only knew the man Moses from his two hours interviewing him and the brief report he had read before the interview. It was enough though for him to realize the two men he was going to help were opposites. One tall and good-looking, the other squat and ugly. One intelligent and quick-witted, the other as thick as a woodpile outside a timber mill. The Commander in Bond's office had explained that although DS Thumper was wanted for the murder of Philip Alliss, neither he nor the AC believed that he was guilty. The Commander did not give any detail about why they thought the two men were collaborating. It still seemed a stretch to the DS. Why would Moses break Thumper's knee and then partner him in an investigation? Not that there was an investigation, not officially. Thumper was chasing Moses because the Brass did not want him to get away with assaulting a police officer. The whole thing was a farce and the DS thought no good would come of it. He was flying to this town called Pozzuoli because Dick Thumper was a friend and he obviously needed help. He knew that the Commander had also kept something from him. He could tell by the lack of eye contact during the briefing.

The flight was not direct to Naples, but landed in Palermo en route, which was not en route, because Palermo was south of Naples and London was northwest. The route turned out to be a long-haul dog-leg, although the airline did not class it as such. Standing was sitting in the cramped space with his knees practically either side of his ears for almost six hours instead of the three it would have taken had the flight been direct. By the time the plane landed in Naples, his knees were screaming and his head felt like an over-inflated beach ball.

Despite the pain, Adam was in deep thought as he walked into the arrivals hall in Capodichino and saw his shadow nemesis waiting on the other side of the barrier. He thought he was going mad until he realized that the man was not the same. He had on the same or a similar Armani suit and the same baseball cap and Ray-Bans, but he was slightly taller than the man he had left in Luton.

The Sergeant did not let on that he had seen his new tail, but just strolled nonchalantly to the bus station outside the arrivals hall and ordered a ticket to Piazza Garibaldi in Naples. The tail did not board the bus, but Adam saw him get into a Fiat Punto and drive out of the airport car park ahead of the bus. He guessed that his tail suspected he would not have been spotted and that the DS would head for the main train station and so drove on to get there first. As soon as the car was out of sight, the DS got off the bus and walked to the taxi rank. He ordered a taxi to Pozzuoli in fluent Italian.

Chapter 18

There was a pile of bent paperclips in front of Inspector Izzo. His frustration had become far more acute in the last forty-eight hours. After losing the Alliss boy, he had also lost the detective from London and now there was a European-wide hunt for him. Apparently, he was wanted for questioning in relation to the murder of someone in a West Kensington apartment.

When the Colonel turned up in the Pozzuoli office for the second time ever that morning, because the English police Assistant Commissioner had called General Barberini asking if the Italian police had any idea of the blond giant's whereabouts, Izzo's day had taken a serious downward turn.

"Izzo, the General was tearing me a new one for nearly an hour!" The Black Cat blurted as he walked into the office without knocking. No preamble, no "Good morning, Pietro". He appeared to be furious that the Englishman seemed to have left the country without their knowledge.

"Have you ever spent an hour on the telephone with General Barberini?" Izzo shook his head. "Believe me, it is not an hour I would wish on you. What happened to the English policeman?"

"You told me to give him a free hand sir, let him conduct his investigation in his own way," Izzo reminded him, which provoked a snort from the Colonel.

"And what of the other one, the one he was chasing?" The Inspector shrugged. There had been intermittent sightings of Moses, but he just seemed to be hanging around the police station in Pozzuoli, as if he expected the Alliss boy to show up there.

"Is that Pompeii incident connected?"

Izzo shook his head. Although there had been reports of a shooting down in Pompeii, there had been no witnesses and it seemed that no one was hurt. Forensics had not uncovered any evidence of a shooting, just a broken pair of Ray-Bans under a pile of litter. As there was no indication of Camorra involvement, the local police were handling it and Pietro failed to see how the Englishmen could have been involved. He would not tell the Colonel he had returned the Glock Forty-Five to the blond giant. It would result in a disciplinary hearing at the very least and possibly even dismissal.

The Colonel finally left with an admonition that amounted to "Get it sorted, now". Inspector Izzo did not know how to proceed. The English Sergeant was nowhere to be found, Cipolle's team was watching the restaurant for signs of the Alliss boy, but whoever had him, they were keeping him well hidden, and Moses was hanging about Pozzuoli in plain view. Hence the new metal menagerie on his desk.

"Pronto," Izzo responded to a heavy rapping on the office door. The desk Sergeant opened it a crack and stuck his face through the gap.

"Sorry to interrupt, sir, your phone is off."

Izzo nodded. "What do you want, Sergeant?"

"There are two Englishmen at the counter in reception. They say they must speak with you."

"Two Englishmen?" Izzo was in shock. He had been worrying paperclips for the last two hours over the disappearance of the detective and if he had heard correctly, he was now in the reception area of the police station. "One blond with very short hair and big muscles who looks like the village idiot, the other bald and really ugly?" The Sergeant nodded.

"Make sure the blond one is unarmed and then show them into my office, Sergeant."

The Inspector welcomed the pair standing behind his rickety desk with open arms. "Gentlemen, welcome." Thumper looked at Moses and shrugged his lack of understanding at the gesture. "How can I be of assistance? Sergeant Cipolle, bring another chair," he shouted through the open door of the office without giving them a chance to respond.

Archie watched as a few moments later a detective in plain clothes walked in carrying two collapsible wooden chairs and offered one to him. Archie took it and Thumper sat on the rickety chair that was already there. Sergeant Cipolle opened the other and stood it against the now closed door, before sitting on it, stretching out his legs and folding his hands across his chest.

"Tell me, gentlemen, how I can be of help to you?" Izzo asked, while smiling the same beatific smile he had used on Archie a couple of days before. Archie was wary of it. The position of the Sergeant, what was it, Cipolle, seemed to indicate that Thumper and himself were actually prisoners of the dapper copper.

"We have some information for you about the Alliss boy." Thumper said, apparently unaware that anything was amiss. The Inspector nodded encouragement for him to continue. "We have reason to believe that he's working with the local Mafia."

"Really, Sergeant, and what makes you believe these reasons?" Izzo already knew that the boy was working with the Camorra. He wanted to know why these two suspected it to be so.

"I spoke to his father yesterday afternoon. It seems that the family is originally from here."

"What is the family name?" Izzo interrupted.

"Elenco." The inspector nodded at the Sergeant, who stood up from his chair and left the room. Izzo was furious. He guessed that The Met already knew that the boy's father had originated in the Naples region. He could not fathom any reason why they would consider it appropriate to withhold that information.

"Please go on, Sergeant."

"It seems that the grandfather of the boy used to work for a mafia family and he ran away with a load of money. There is some family rift between father and son, so the son is rebelling."

"What? The lawyer and his father, or the lawyer and his son?" Izzo interrupted again.

"The lawyer, Philip and his son, Christopher." Izzo nodded. "It seems the man left the boy and his mother, because he decided that he was a poof..."

Izzo interrupted again, "What is poof, please?"

"Oh, um, a gay. A homosexual." The inspector nodded his understanding. "The boy didn't take it too well and then his mother died unexpectedly."

Izzo felt he understood the young Alliss's reaction. He could not profess any knowledge about the way marriages seemed to work, or more specifically fail, in other parts of Europe. His own marriage had failed, but that was because he was married to the job. To think that a man would leave the mother of his children for another man, just did not add up for Izzo. If the guy felt he was gay, sure play the field a little, but do not abandon your familial responsibilities.

"After the death of the mother," Thumper continued, "what had been reticence turned into open hostility." Philip Alliss had spoken about the late-night phone calls where he could hear breathing but nobody would speak and the postcards from different places, which at best were rude and at worst highly insulting.

"Could that hostility have become violence?" Izzo asked.

"I asked the same of Philip Alliss. He seems to think not. His boy is, as he put it, all wind and piss..."

"Please, what does it mean, all wind and piss?"

"It means he uses a lot of words and gestures, but would not have it in him to commit a violent act." The Inspector nodded his understanding.

"In Italian, we say "belle parole non pascon i gatti", nice words don't feed the cats." Thumper did not think it meant the same thing at all, but let it slide. If Izzo thought he understood what was meant, that was all that mattered. At that moment, Cipolle returned to the office and whispered something in the Inspector's ear before replacing his seat in front of the closed office door.

"Please continue, Sergeant," the Inspector said.

"Philip Alliss thinks the boy is here to cause trouble. He also thinks that he will be in trouble himself."

"Why are you men here, though?"

"We came to tell you the information I got from Philip Alliss when I went to London yesterday."

"No, I mean why have you not left Naples? What is there for you here now?"

Archie responded. "Mr Alliss wants us to locate and protect his son."

"I think at this point, gentlemen, your mission is over."

"Why do you say that," Archie asked?

"The older Alliss is dead." Izzo spoke bluntly because he wanted to evoke some reaction from the two men. Specifically, from the Sergeant. If they had prior knowledge that Alliss had been tortured and murdered in his kitchen, their reactions would be feigned, perhaps over-acted, definitely not natural. He was not surprised when both men blanched and looked horrified at the news.

"But I was only speaking to him yesterday," the Sergeant blurted.

"Yes Sergeant, and that is why there is a problem." Izzo watched as the Sergeant shook his head and looked bemused. "Philip Alliss was found with his throat cut. He had been tortured. His body was discovered yesterday afternoon and you were seen entering and leaving the apartment yesterday afternoon."

Izzo watched the Sergeant, looking for an indication that he was somehow involved in the killing. There was none. His lower jaw seemed to have become detached from whatever it was that held his mouth closed, because his mouth was so wide open it must have hurt.

"I left him in one piece!" Thumper blurted. He looked at Archie, who sat there betraying no emotion. "You must believe me, Archie, he was okay when I left him."

Archie turned and winked at him with a smile. The DS suddenly felt a gratitude of a type he had never felt before towards this man. Not even to Layla the night she claimed his virginity, all those long years before.

"I must say," Izzo said, "that I am not very ready to think you are the killing man that they claim. But, I must arrest you because there is a warrant for you in the international police communications network." He shrugged to emphasise that it was out of his control. Thumper shrugged and stood, allowing the

Sergeant by the door to take him by the shoulder and lead him away from the room.

As he walked out of the door he turned and said, "See if you can find out what's going on, Archie, will you?"

"Course, Dick. I will have you out in a jiffy."

Chapter 19

"Sir, I have a June Whiting from the Evening Herald on line one," Margery announced through the intercom.

"Okay Margery, I will take it," the AC sighed. He was preparing for the emergency war room meeting called by the Commissioner because of the situation in Naples, and could do without the interruption. "Bond."

"Assistant Commissioner, I am June Whiting and I have the Met desk at the Evening Herald."

"Yes, Ms Whiting, how can I help you?"

"My editor asked me to make contact and ask if you have any comment on a story we are about to go to print with this evening."

"Which story is that, Ms Whiting?"

"Well it seems that one of your police officers was assaulted in Roper's last Friday night and suffered a broken knee?"

"I have no comment on that story," Bond said, before hanging up. He flipped the switch on the office intercom, before saying, "No interruptions, Margery."

"Yes, sir. I mean, no, sir!"

Bond stood up and walked over to his door. He listened with his ear pressed to the panelling for several seconds. He was satisfied that he could hear the clicking of Margery's keypad before returning to his desk and calling a number on his mobile phone.

"What is it, Detective?"

The call from Ms Whiting of the Evening Herald had been a ruse that he and DS Standing had agreed during their meeting the day before. While abroad, the Sergeant would be unable to call the Assistant Commissioner other than from a call box and the cost of phoning the AC's mobile from a call box would have been impractical. The woman who called the office was a friend of the Detective's. She believed the call to be some sort of a practical joke. The situation with the newspaper was a fabrication, although a Ms Whiting did have the Met desk. If anyone had been listening in to the call, they might become suspicious when a story did not appear in the Herald, but it was not likely. Reporters were constantly fishing with small amounts of information with which their editors then later refused to run.

"I've been compromised."

"What? How?"

"Don't ask me how, sir, because I don't know, but there was someone waiting for me in my hotel yesterday afternoon."

"What sort of someone?"

"Let's just say that his skin tone was not far off the colour of Extra Vergine olive oil. And he had an accomplice here in Naples, too."

"You're sure?"

"The two of them were like peas in a pod…"

"What, like twins?" Bond interrupted.

"Could be, but my guess is they are just two weirdos with very similar fetishes. There must be a leak somewhere in your office."

Bond thought about it briefly. He supposed the Detective Sergeant to be right. There was no other explanation. "So, what is it that you propose we do?"

"Before we can do very much, sir, we need to discover where the leak is. If they know our moves at the same time as we know them ourselves, this operation is doomed."

"I agree."

"What was agreed yesterday was I would enlist the aid of Moses and go in search of DS Thumper. But from what I can gather on the Italian news, Thumper has already been arrested."

"Yes, I was going to tell you when you called in later with your status report. They arrested him yesterday. There are two special branch guys from the Embassy in Rome going to pick him up tomorrow."

"Okay, we need to contrive something with the Italian detective so that whoever is leaking information, they feel compelled to inform their paymasters."

"But, Sergeant, it could be anyone."

"I don't think so, sir. How many knew that I was in your office yesterday?"

"Pretty much everyone who saw you sitting outside in the armchair, I would guess."

"Okay, granted. But how many people knew I would be in Luton airport?"

There was a lengthy pause at the end of the line. Eventually the AC said, "You, commander Blythe, and me."

"That narrows the field a little."

"I cannot believe that Derek Blythe has sold out to the enemy."

"We will soon find out," the Sergeant said.

"What do you propose?"

"It is my guess that someone framed DS Thumper to get him out of the way."

"Why would they do that? He is a bodyguard, not a detective."

"But do they know that? I think they saw a British police officer arrive on the scene when they were neck deep in whatever they are doing and decided to get rid of him."

"I am afraid I don't buy it, Sergeant. I don't think that the sequence of events really tallies with your theory. If there is a mole, they must know that Thumper is a protection officer and they must have told whoever it is there in Italy of that fact, surely?"

Standing frowned into the telephone. He knew Bond was right, but was wracking his brains to think of some way to use the Thumper situation to smoke out the mole.

"They know that Moses is here though, I'm guessing?"

"Yes, apparently. They threatened to take a pot shot at him at some sort of meeting he interrupted in Pompeii."

"And you know that because…?"

"The Italian Inspector called me with the information when he arrested Thumper."

"So why don't we leak it that Thumper has been cleared of all charges and is being released."

"How will that help our situation?"

"My guess is that they will follow Thumper and attempt to neutralize him. Getting rid of the fly in their soup, so to speak."

"Will that not be putting DS Thumper at risk?"

"I'll keep tabs on Thumper and intercept any threats to his person. We can also get the Inspector to provide us with some support."

"Okay, Detective. I don't like it but I don't think we have much alternative."

"Something else, sir."

"What is it?"

"The man who followed me was a professional. Commander Blythe intimated some sort of Mafia connection, but my experience of the Mafia is they are keen amateurs and not terribly professional."

The AC frowned at the portrait of the Queen and decided to tell the DS about the suspected involvement of the Red Brigade. Not that he thought they would be any more professional than Standing thought the mafia to be, but because he did not really understand his own motives in holding the information back.

"Is Thumper armed?" Standing asked when the AC had finished explaining about the call that GCHQ had intercepted.

"He had a weapon with him. I don't suppose he still has it, seeing as he is in a cell. I will talk to this Izzo character and ask him to return it when he releases him."

‡

Izzo frowned at his scampi as a stranger pulled up a chair opposite and sat down without preamble. The Inspector raised an eyebrow questioningly, but said nothing.

"Inspector Izzo?" the stranger asked. Pietro nodded.

"Bene! Do you mind?" he asked in fluent Italian pointing at a breadstick. Izzo shrugged his acquiescence. "I'm here at the request of Assistant Commissioner Bond. I think you know who I mean?" Izzo nodded.

"I believe you have an English police Sergeant in detention and you plan to hand him over to two special branch detectives tomorrow?" Izzo nodded again.

"Assistant Commissioner Bond is going to call you when you are back at your desk with a different proposal. The Sergeant had nothing to do…"

"What is your name?" Izzo interrupted. He did not know why this man was here, and that needed to be discussed, but he thought that it would be polite for him to at least introduce himself before handing out instructions.

"My name does not matter, but you can call me Buddy, if you feel it is important." There was no real reason for Standing to remain incognito. He said it more through habit than anything. He had spent so much time investigating organized crime as an undercover operative, that staying unknown had become second nature, an instinct which kept him alive.

Izzo looked at the man across the table. He could tell that he was a professional and that he was not Italian. Although his spoken language was fluent, there was an accent to it that was not mother tongue.

"So, I am supposed to believe you without question?" Izzo asked, also in Italian.

The stranger looked at him for a while before responding, "I think you would recognize the accent of Assistant Commissioner Bond?" the man asked. Izzo nodded.

"He will be calling your desk in thirty minutes. You don't have to believe me, but you can listen to him and make a decision based upon that."

"And what is it that he will say?"

"I think it best for AC Bond to explain himself."

The inspector nodded and returned to his meal. He knew that he did not need to accept the word of this man, nor indeed from the Assistant Commissioner who had called before, but his curiosity was piqued. From what he knew of the blond giant in the cells, which was admittedly little, he did not believe the man to be capable of murder, nor stupid enough to traipse into the Pozzuoli police station with a fantastical story when he was wanted for that murder. Dumb, yes, but not that dumb. No one was that dumb, surely?

"Okay Mr Stranger, I will do as you ask."

"Thank you, Inspector. You are doing us a great service."

"Where can I reach you?"

"I will stay here and eat something. I am very hungry. If you want to help the ACSO, you will find me here for the next hour or so."

Chapter 20

Thumper was lying on the metal cot in his cell in Pozzuoli station with his hands behind his head. He was thinking about the call he had made to Layla when he landed at Luton, feeling a need to keep his mind away from Kensington and the mental image of Philip Alliss, naked and bleeding.

The wall of patience he had built up as a defence against Layla's controlling nature was finally crumbling. He loved his sons, but there is only so much controlling a man can stomach before rebelling. If he was to be honest with himself, he married Layla because she took his virginity and he mistook that lustful gratitude for love. Earlier in the week the D-word had flashed through his mind fleetingly, but now it was an ever-present nagging in his frontal lobe. A nagging that was as persistent as the nagging that had caused it.

"Where are you?" she had asked, without so much as a 'How are you?'

He told her he was in Pozzuoli, having decided during the flight that he would not tell her he was back in England. She would have made his life hell if she had found out that he had left the Fiat in the south of Italy to fly home. But worse still, she would have castrated him if she had found out he had taken money from little more than a stranger to do so.

"Where?"

"Pozzuoli, near Naples in the South of Italy."

"What are you doing there?"

Thumper had almost felt a sense of gratitude that Layla was showing some interest in his work. He told her that he could not talk about it, before she revealed the real reason she had asked. "I need the Fiat back. I can't park the Toyota when I go shopping, not enough room. Where is it? I have my keys so I can get a taxi and collect it."

"The Fiat is in Naples," he stuttered. "With me." He only just caught himself revealing that he was not in the south of Italy.

"You drove my Fiat all the way to Naples? What gives you the right?" she screamed.

It was then that he dropped the receiver back into its cradle and cursed the day he had signed the register in that little backroom behind the altar. He needed to take a serious look at his marriage. He could not sustain it in its current form, because he felt he would not be responsible for his actions were it to continue in the same vein.

He was very tired. He had not slept during the night. Despite his best efforts, grizzly images of the grey-haired, manicured man with his gorge in his lap kept popping into his mind. Izzo had not provided any detail, but Thumper's imagination kept it playing over and over in his mind, driving him to wakefulness.

Thumper had been in the cell now for almost two days, arrested on suspicion of murder. Murder! Him! Dick Thumper had never so much as squashed a spider, never mind murdered anyone. He had been amazed in Pompeii when he pulled the trigger to shoot the would-be murderer, and thought it was probably his training and the shot was instinct. But torturing a man to death? How could Dugs have let the others believe that Dick Thumper was capable of torture and cold-blooded murder? Surely the Super knew him better than that? He was beginning to think that continued service in The Met was no longer viable, that the D-word applied to more than just his marriage. When he got out of this mess he would seriously consider a career shift. He was not sure what he could do other than protect the Royal Family, because he had no experience in anything else, but he could not see himself working for The Met much longer.

The Detective's thoughts were interrupted by the clatter of someone turning the key in the lock of his cell. He swung around to see who was coming and jumped up, pleasantly surprised, when Detective Sergeant Adam Standing walked in, closely followed by Inspector Izzo.

"Adam."

'Ah, Adam,' Izzo thought.

"Dick."

The men shook hands with the genuine warmth of two who have known each other a long time and feel a mutual respect.

"What's going on?" Thumper asked.

"Bond sent me to find you and find out what's happening."

"Happening where?"

"Here. Why are you and Bald Archie working together?"

"What about the murder?" Standing could hear the resentment in his friend's voice. He knew where it was coming from. He too would feel betrayed if his governor had thought him capable of murder.

"No one really thinks you murdered anyone, Dick. They put the APW out because they needed to talk to you."

"So, what's changed?"

"Before you were arrested, I was to come over and make contact with Archie. We guessed you two are working together."

"Okay, but surely my arrest meant you no longer needed to track me down. So why are you here?"

"The ACSO is really upset. He has given priority to the apprehension of whoever is responsible for the death of the lawyer Philip Alliss."

"When I left London just over a week ago, the priority was to punish Archie for daring to assault a police officer."

Standing frowned. In his opinion, everything that Superintendent Douglas had ordered Thumper to do after the incident in the club was a mistake. Conducting a vendetta against a citizen with all the checks and balances now in place would probably lead to an investigation and disciplinary action, if not criminal proceedings. He would not want to be Dugs for all the diamonds in South Africa.

"From what I can gather, Dick, that was Dugs. Bond and Rogers-Smythe did not seem too happy about it. But they do want the bastards who killed Philip Alliss. They've no interest in continuing the vendetta against Moses."

"So, I can go home, then?"

"Well, sure you could, but I need some help first."

"I thought you came here to find me?"

"Initially that was the case, like I said. But now Bond wants me to see if I can help the Italians solve the murder."

"What makes them think the murder can be solved in Pozzuoli?" Thumper frowned his incomprehension. The murder took place in Kensington. What possible connection could there be with Southern Italy.

"I was tailed in Luton and someone was waiting for me when I arrived at Capodichino airport. It must be related to the murder. Why else would they tail me?"

Thumper nodded, before thinking of something else. "How did they know you were going to be at Luton airport?"

"We think there is a leak. That's where you come in."

"How can I help with a leak?"

"We're going to use you as bait to draw out the mole."

"What about the Alliss boy?" Thumper did not want to abandon the self-imposed objective that Archie and he had agreed. It was an "egg in your face" gesture to the senior officers who had sent him on this witch hunt.

"If we can save him too, that will be a bonus, but our priority is justice for Alliss Senior and plugging the leak."

"That might be your priority, Adam, me and Archie have a different idea."

"Look, Dick, just help me with this one thing, and then I will help you save the kid, okay?" Thumper looked at his friend for a few seconds before reaching a decision.

"I will talk to Archie."

"Thanks, Dick."

"So, what happens now?"

"The ACSO is going to release a circular in The Yard saying that you've been released and no longer suspected of the murder. My guess is whoever killed Alliss want you out of the picture."

"I'm a protection officer. Why would they want me out of the picture?"

"That is a mystery, but something has them riled up. The torture of Alliss was probably meant as a message of some description."

"Okay, I can see that. How are we going to play this?"

"If anything happens after they let you go, we should be able to uncover the leak."

"Okay, so I'm the goat staked out for the tyrannosaurus." Adam looked at Dick then, surprised at the depth of the statement, little realizing that Thumper had recently taken his sons to see a movie about a theme park full of dinosaurs.

"Don't worry, Dick. Me and the Inspector have got your back."

Romano and Fabio were given the job on the fly. The Fratelli Sconosciuti, called that by the other soldiers because they were literally unknown brothers, were too busy to take on anything else. All that the family knew about them was that they were brothers and favourites of the Capo, Mama Cucciolo. The family soldiers did not know what the Fratelli were doing, only that it was so important to the boss that she had them doing nothing else. Mama had called Romano and Fabio to the restaurant in Posillipo earlier that morning, praised them for their past achievements, and told them that if they were successful with this job, they would have the rest of the year off with their feet up on Pantelleria, where the family kept several villas and girls to keep them occupied and happy.

Both men were excited. Several months on Pantelleria being pampered by the exotic women that Mama supplied for the gratification of her soldiers, was not something they took lightly. It was more than that, though. Were they to succeed, and they fully expected to succeed, they would be made for life. Taking on a task where Mama herself had called them to the restaurant, was a great achievement already. To fail would be a catastrophe, though.

The target was a big dumb blond English police officer and a short, ugly, bald man who was some sort of a bodyguard. Neither of them was thought to be particularly dangerous. They were to follow the dumb one and shoot them both when they came into contact. Easy.

Romano stood up from the tree he was lounging against in front of the police station and dropped his cigarette at his feet. The big blond police officer had sauntered out of the station and was ambling between the palm trees in the little park without a care. Romano could not really tell, not from this distance, but he seemed to be whistling. From what Romano knew, the man had been in the cells for a couple of days and had somehow made Mama mad enough to want him dead. Here he was whistling in the street like some demented street urchin, causing Romano to smile. Easy.

It got even better when Romano watched the man climb into a pink Fiat 500 that was parked in one of the spaces on Maria Sacchini. He seemed to fold himself double just to get in behind the steering wheel. Romano laughed, wolf-whistled and waved at Fabio to bring up the car.

"Have you seen that Cazzo?" he asked as Fabio pulled up.

"Yeah, it's going to be like stealing a handbag from a little old lady on Corso Umberto," Fabio replied with feeling, because it evoked good memories of his adolescence.

Dick Thumper drove the Fiat to Posillipo. He expected Archie would be there, keeping tabs on the restaurant, because it was the only place where they had seen the Alliss boy. He knew it was a bit loose, but believed there would be no other choice. Archie had promised to get Dick out of the Italian nick, and the only way to do that would be to find the boy and somehow solve the murder of Alliss Senior. Chris Alliss was the key to that crime and the restaurant was the key to the boy.

Thumper kept his eyes to the front as he drove down the coastal road to Posillipo. The urge was to keep looking over his shoulder to see if he was being tailed, but he knew that would only give the game away. His other urge was to look for Adam Standing, but he knew that too would give the game away. He needed to trust his friend and the Italian detective if this ruse was to have any chance of success. None of that made it any easier though. He kept thinking of the scene in the movie where the white goat was staked out for the T-Rex to swallow.

He knew the Fiat would be conspicuous, so he parked it in the car park of the Pausilipon Children's hospital with the intention of walking along Via Posillipo to the restaurant. He looked at the silhouette of the volcano as he walked out of the car park gate. It presented a menacing presence that dominated the landscape behind the city and over the bay. He ducked into a gift shop a short way from the car park and bought a cap and a pair of cheap plastic sunglasses.

Thumper guessed Archie would not be far from La Orchidea and that he would be hidden. Archie had been seen in Pompeii, however fleetingly, so he needed to stay out of sight if he was to succeed. Thumper tried to crouch down as much as possible to disguise his height as he walked along the main street into the area where the restaurant was located. He guessed that the Mafia boys would know him to be a tall blond haired Englishman, so with his hair covered and his height hidden, he hoped he could remain undetected.

As he neared the entrance to the restaurant, he ducked down a side street, thinking that Archie might choose to watch the back for any signs of Alliss Junior. He supposed that the comings and goings of the Mafia boys would be clandestine after the Pompeii incident.

He was standing looking at the back door to the restaurant, judging by the piles of rotting food in the two skips beside it, when he felt a tap on his shoulder. Thumper spun around, reaching for the Glock in his shoulder holster, only to see Archie grinning at him from what appeared to be the entrance of a very seedy hotel.

"What the fuck, Archie," he whispered as his pulse began to slow to something resembling normal male adult rates.

"Why are you whispering?"

"Dunno, I guess I am on edge. What's happening?"

"Not here, let's go up to the room."

Thumper nodded and had just turned to follow Archie into the hotel when he heard, "Don't even think about it, Dick wad!"

Romano watched as the giant parked his car in the hospital car park and bought a hat and sunglasses from the gift shop. He thought about calling Mama. It was a little worrying that the man drove to Posillipo, where the family restaurant was located, but even more worrying that he disguised himself before walking into the town. What stopped Romano from making the call was the promise of glory were he and Fabio able to see the task through without intervention from anyone else. Instead of calling Mama, he called Fabio. "You follow on the other side of the street."

"Okay. What do you think he's doing here?" Fabio's tone was worried. Romano did not blame him for worrying, but knew they would succeed anyway. They would not be able to shoot them here, not so close to the restaurant, but they could kidnap them and kill them somewhere else.

"The ugly one must be here. Let's just get them and worry about why they are here afterwards. We can take them to Afragola and make them talk."

"Why don't we call Mama first?"

"If we call Mama, she will send out others. We can kiss goodbye to the African Figs then."

"Okay, okay."

"You walk the other side. Keep your eyes on me." Romano clicked off his phone and watched the man walk as though he had dumped a load in his pants. He shook his head and smiled to himself as he sauntered down Via Posillipo at a respectable distance. He picked up his pace as his quarry ducked down Villa de Martino, just before reaching the restaurant. He waved at Fabio to keep on going on the other side of the street and followed as the man moved to stand beside the entrance to the Hotel Sunshine and look at the rear door that led to the kitchens.

Romano nearly jumped for joy when he saw the squat ugly one appear in the door of the seedy hotel and tap the tall one on the shoulder. As he picked up his pace and pulled the gun from the back of his trousers, he began to think of how best to carry out their mission. It would not be advisable to shoot the two men here, not so close to the family premises. He knew that others in the crew would shoot first and ask questions later, including the Sconosciuti, but he would show Mama that he was made of better stuff. As he neared, the two men turned their backs to him and made to go into the hotel. Fabio had moved past and was now approaching them from the opposite side. Romano raised his gun and was just about to tell the men to stand still when he felt the cold touch of steel on his neck and heard, "Don't even think about it, Dick wad!" Romano did not speak English, but the feel of cold steel was a universal language. Without moving he shifted his eyes to see where his partner was. He could see that the police detective, Izzo, was crouching over his supine body with his gun pointing at his forehead and cuffs in his hand.

"Okay, you're sure," Bond asked, before hanging up his mobile phone. Standing's ruse had failed. Commander Blythe had been the only other person who knew that Standing was travelling to Italy through Luton. No one else had known. The commander's mobile phone and his work phone had both been tapped, and the

Commander himself was under surveillance. During the operation, the Commander had been in Hammersmith town hall as a guest speaker at a Neighbourhood Watch meeting. He had not left the stage or use his phone at any point during the course of the sting.

Forgetting himself, Bond picked up his landline receiver and dialled DS Standing's mobile number. It was only on the third ring that Standing answered.

"I guess we know who it is, as you are ringing from the landline?"

"Oh shit! Sorry, wrong number," Bond said. He heard Standing's line go dead and sat with the receiver at his ear, hesitating, angry at himself for making such a fundamental error. It was because of that error though that he heard the click and everything came tumbling into place. When they had been discussing who might have leaked information, they spoke about who knew he had been at Luton airport where the tail first appeared. DS Standing, Commander Bond, and the AC himself were the only people they considered. But there had been a fourth person. A person who none of them would even notice, because they were just so much background noise in an already noisy environment.

The AC clicked the intercom into the on position, "Margery, can you come in here for a moment, please."

Chapter 21

Christopher Alliss had a problem.

It had all seemed like a game when he first called the number in Posillipo, just after he was sacked from the pig's foot in Eindhoven by that pompous French dick, van den Hemmel. He got very drunk in the Kaffee De Groot that night and rang the number on the inside cover of the old diary he had found in the box of crap under the stairs of the family home; the family home where his mother had died suddenly while his father was fraternising with his boyfriend in the Kensington apartment. He would hate his father forever because of that, but he was now wondering if he had done the right thing in coming here to Italy and bringing the diary with him.

He had never seen the diary before the day he found it while he was throwing out his mother's old things after selling the house. Mother left her estate to him and he sold the family home to get up Alliss Senior's nose. He had not known there was anything of his father's still in the house. He thought he had thrown it all out after the betrayal. It seemed like he had missed under the stairs, though.

When he opened the diary, he did not recognize any of the names or numbers, but he knew that it involved the old life of which his father refused to speak. Drunk on Jenever, he decided he would use it to wind the old git up, and dialled one of the numbers on the inside cover. Some old lady had answered in Italian, and rather than hang up he had made himself known. She spoke to him in okay English and asked him how he came by the number. Although they spoke for several minutes, the next day he had no recollection of the call. He was reminded of it a couple of days later when two Italians in Armani suits wearing shades and baseball caps sat down at his table and asked if he was Christopher Alliss. They looked remarkably like twins, but when Alliss asked, they said they were just good friends.

They plied him with drinks and said they were from the old country near Pozzuoli and were friends of his father's family. They asked if they could see the diary where he had found the number. And when, apparently happy with the authenticity of it, they said that there were cousins who were dying to meet him and that he should come to Pozzuoli and say hello if he ever got the chance, he said he would. He watched them leave, both bumping into the table as they walked past the bar, because they were too dick to remove their sunglasses in a darkened hole like the Groot. He never expected to hear from them again, and was very surprised when Arrie called up to his room with a postcard from Italy the following week.

The postcard was blunt and to the point. "Come to Pozzuoli, take the train, tell no one, and bring it with you".

He did not remember the conversation in the bar, or even if the two dicks in Armani suits had even told him their names, but he supposed he had promised to visit his family in the old country. He should have been nervous about it and thought long and hard and then carried on his simple existence in Eindhoven, spending his inheritance. But rather than being nervous, he felt a sense of adventure and perhaps a little drive to get even further up his father's nose. The same morning that Arrie gave him the postcard, he packed his small bag and left for Eindhoven station to enquire about trains to Naples.

When he got to Pozzuoli near Naples, the family put him to work washing dishes in their restaurant and told him he needed to register in the local cop shop to be legal. He worked in the restaurant during the lunchtime trade and ate there in the evenings, before taking a beer with the sous-chef, Ricci. It was all innocuous until Mama Cucciolo asked him to help Ricci on a quick job one night after he had been there about a week.

They collected a couple of loaded black industrial bin-liners from a garage near the restaurant and dumped them in the back of the van that was used to collect fish from Pozzuoli market each morning. The bags were heavily bound with black masking tape and the van smelt strongly of rotting fish, so Chris convinced himself there was nothing sinister about the contents.

When they dumped them at four in the morning in the foyer of a building on a little island over a bridge, he said to himself that it was just rubbish and they were doing a bit of fly tipping to keep the restaurant business costs down. In his heart, he knew that was not the truth. Ricci told him to wait in the van while he "unwrapped" the parcels and laughed when he used a craft knife to cut away the plastic and Chris had to fight against his gag reflex from the passenger seat because of the smell.

After the trip to the island, Chris told himself he had not seen anything out of the ordinary and the smell was just the fish. The next day he carried on washing dishes in the restaurant as if nothing had happened. It was when the stranger in the baseball cap tried to shoot the ugly English guy in Pompeii that Chris began to feel he might have made a mistake. Despite trying to act all macho when the man blundered into their meeting, he felt a pang of remorse about how he had treated his father. He never expected Alliss Senior to send a Private Eye to rescue him and it was touching.

There was no way he could pretend fly tipping on that day. Ricci said they were going to meet a man from the Brigata Rossa, which meant nothing to Chris, but when they drove out of the city and went into Pompeii, he became suspicious. The man they met under the arch made him break into a sweat. Ricci said that he was to help this man on a job as a favour to Mama Cucciolo. Chris had looked at him and thought there was something about the man that seemed vaguely familiar. He had felt uncomfortable under the archway and had taken the decision he should have taken after the incident on the island. He decided to tell Ricci that he was returning to the UK and so would not be able to help this man with whatever it was they planned. Just when he opened his mouth to speak, the ugly bald white man came stumbling in on them.

"Chris, Chris Alliss?" he had asked. Chris had almost felt a sense of relief to have a compatriot arrive on the scene. He was obviously English, not only because of his skin tone, but also because of the way he dressed and his accent. When the vaguely familiar Italian pulled a gun from the waistband of his trousers and pointed it at the Englishman with a feral grin, Chris froze and squeezed his eyes shut. He opened them after the shot, expecting to see a corpse at his feet. Instead, the man who had pulled the gun was clutching his right shoulder and grimacing with pain. His sunglasses and gun were in the dust at his feet.

"Help, quick," Ricci said, "Help me get him away from here." As they had taken one shoulder each and assisted the man out of the tunnel, Chris looked back. The Englishman was standing where he had been, motionless. Chris could not see how the strange Italian had been shot, there was no gun, no smoke, nothing. The ugly Englishman had just been standing there with his eyes shut.

After the shooting, they left the man in a baseball cap at a villa in Afragola, a town close to Naples, and returned to the restaurant. Ricci spoke to Mama in their fast and unintelligible local dialect for several minutes before she told Chris that he and Ricci would need to go and hide in case there was any comeback from the shooting in Pompeii. She had her arm around his shoulders and was guiding him towards the rear door to the restaurant when Chris told her he had decided to return to

England. There was a fleeting look of pure hatred on her face before she masked it with a smile and said, "Sure, but do this for me for now. When the heat dies, then you go. Okay?" Chris nodded and allowed himself to be led away and driven to the villa in Afragola.

When he went to the kitchen to get some breakfast the following morning, Ricci and the wounded stranger were not there. They had been replaced by two middle-aged men who spoke no English and carried wicked-looking, sawn off shotguns. He had not paid much attention as he ate his breakfast on the veranda. Later in the day, though, he could see that the villa was surrounded by a tall wall with a large metal gate in the front. There was broken glass cemented into the top and Chris just knew that if he tried to open the gate it would be locked.

That had been two days before. Now he was sitting on the veranda eating a lunch of cured ham, melon and rustic Italian bread. He was extremely nervous and trying not to show it. When he had strolled casually by the gate the previous day, one of the guards he called Tweedledum and Tweedledee, waved his shotgun emphatically and warned him away. It was obvious to Chris then, that he was a prisoner in this villa in the hinterland of Naples. He could not escape, and if he did, he had nowhere to go. He knew that the town was near Naples, but he guessed that the backdrop to the city would be where the organized crime families would be concentrated. He did not doubt that he would not get any further than a few metres before being apprehended.

His thoughts were interrupted when he heard the lock in the metal gate turn. The doors were thrown open and two Land Rovers that looked suspiciously like British military vehicles, were driven into the complex. If possible, Chris became even more nervous when two men wearing identical baseball caps climbed out from the driver's seats of the two vehicles. One was the same man who had been shot in Pompeii. The other looked very like him, and it was when they were standing together beside the land Rovers that Chris realized he had seen them before. These were the two nameless men who had come to him in Eindhoven.

Just then, the gate opened again and Ricci rode a big engined Cagiva trial bike into the complex. Chris was glad to see a familiar face as Ricci walked over with the men, who were still in their Armani suits and Ray-Ban sunglasses.

"Chris, these are friends of Mama's. Now we will discuss the job that you are going to help with."

"Hey Ricci, I told Mama I need to get back to England. I need to see my father."

Ricci smiled and shook his head. "I'm sorry, that that will not be possible." He then said something rapidly to one of the grinning men who nodded and took a photograph out of the inside pocket of his suit jacket and handed it over to Chris.

"You know this man?" Ricci asked.

Chris stared at the photo for a long time, unable to recognize who the man was. He recognized the kitchen alright. It was the kitchen in West Kensington that Chris hated so much. That could not possibly be his father, surely? But as he stared at the photo he realized that it was indeed his father. The head was down, but the grey curls in which his father took so much pride were evident.

"This is your father, yes?" Chris nodded, as uncontrollable tears welled up in the corners of his eyes. When, in a drunken stupor, he had phoned the number on the inside cover of the diary, he had not wanted any harm to come to his father. He wanted to hurt him, sure, but not physically. He had wanted his father to feel the same pain that he was feeling.

"Imagine, we will do much worse to you if you do not help in our plans. And do not think to escape. Your father was not safe from us in his Kensington apartment, so we will find you wherever you run."

"What is it you want from me?" Alliss whined.

Ricci turned away and smiled. The boy was weak, and would be easily pliable. Anyone with any street craft would have been aware that his captors needed something and that until they got it, he would remain indispensable. Christopher Alliss had been raised with a silver spoon in his mouth and had no idea how to react to his current circumstance. He would do what Mama and the New Red Brigade needed.

Ricci thought that the family was helping the New Red Brigade achieve their first strike since the major collapse in the eighties. The old crew had suffered a terminal setback in the early eighties and they were all but destroyed. The survivors wanted to atone for that defeat and believed the late nineties was the best time for a resurgence. There were no longer any extreme left wing factions in Italy and so the Brigade was formed to fill the void. They wanted to achieve notoriety with an almighty bang and felt that a high-profile target would provide.

The biggest issue they had was a lack of the necessary resources to carry out any sort of plot. Ricci knew that they had approached the family because the Cuccioli did have those resources. Well, most of them, anyway. Chris represented the final element in the plot, an English speaker without a record and an unrecognizable face.

The boy made to return the photo to Ricci. "No, you keep it as a souvenir," he said, grinning.

Chapter 22

Maresciallo Capo (Sergeant Major) Umberto Falco did not mind being in the Guardia di Finanza, the Italian military customs and excise department. It was a role that he grew into when he was conscripted into the military at the age of eighteen. Over the years, he had enjoyed the sense of purpose the job provided, a sense of purpose that had been sadly lacking during his early youth in Bari where work was hard to come by and criminality rife. So much so, he had signed on for a further twenty years after his two-year term ended.

He had never married, but felt it was a good life even so. He travelled all over Italy guarding both the land and the sea borders of the country he loved. The people showed him some respect wherever he went. Most of the people, anyway. His time guarding the border crossing with Slovenia, up near the small town of Gorizia, was not bad. Many thought it to be a no-hope posting that would never see any action, but Umberto liked that. He was in the nineteenth year of his twenty-year term and he craved a quiet life in the lead up to his retirement. Only a year to go before he could settle down in Bari and concentrate on an existence of off-shore fishing and taking it easy. He had already bought the boat, La

Scamorza, so he would not even need to use his pension fund. That brought a smile to his face. Freedom and riches, what more did any man need?

So what if it was a quiet posting? Not being stressed by working in a part of Italy that few people knew about and even fewer visited was all part of the make-up. It was okay, he thought. No, more than okay, it was ideal on most occasions. Sure, there was the odd time when things might get a bit hairy, but that was true of any job, surely?

Falco sat with his feet up on the desk, thinking about it in the early hours of this Monday morning. The bunker was dense with that level of dark that comes after the moon has set but before the sun has managed to breach the horizon with early light. He was alone, because his partner, Brigadiere Capo (Staff Sergeant) Cantulo had called in sick, which of course meant he was away visiting his wife's family in Turin. It was not a problem. They often covered for each other on the weekend midnight shift.

As a rule, the traffic in the very early hours of a weekend morning was light enough to be termed non-existent. For some reason, this was to be an early morning where that rule did not apply. Umberto was dozing slightly when some instinct jerked him awake. He saw a light dancing on the walls of the guard house, opposite the desk where his feet were propped. He stood up and peered through the narrow slit in the concrete to see that the light was caused by the headlights of an approaching vehicle. He sighed, put on his hat and stepped out of the bunker to stand behind the red and white barrier that marked the limit of Italian territory. During normal daylight hours, he would lift the barrier and wave the vehicle through, but it was unusual for anyone to cross the border at this hour on a Monday morning, so he decided to keep the barrier down and ask for the identification of whoever it was. That was a mistake that Umberto did not live to regret. When he left the barrier in place, the vehicle, rather than slowing down, increased its speed. He could see nothing but headlights and deep shadows behind them. He instinctively drew his service revolver and fired a shot into the air as a warning, but the headlights and the shadows behind just kept coming, faster and faster towards the barrier.

Convinced that they were not going to stop, that they were not just a couple of kids on a jolly, he crouched into the regulation stance, feet apart, knees slightly bent with both hands on his weapon and emptied his clip into the oncoming vehicle. His shots had no effect and he was frowning in frustration when it crashed the barrier and he was thrown against the building from which he had emerged when the headlights had first appeared only moments before.

🔫

Izzo's desk was, unusually, paperclip free and the ashtray carried only a couple of butts. He could not recall a time when his worries had been so few as to allow him to keep his fingers still and his lungs breathing normally. It was as if releasing the village idiot from the cells had liberated his soul in some way. Sure, the senior echelons of The Met had decided that he had had no part in the death of the lawyer in London. Decided by the same people who had put out an arrest order on him, but Izzo's superiors did not know that. They had decided to keep the information to a minimum until they had discovered where the information leak was and now they knew, Izzo was holding back imparting the information because of some sense of superiority over the Colonel.

Assistant Commissioner Bond had been quite clear about that. Not that Izzo was in any way obliged to follow the lead of the English police officer, but truth be told, he was intrigued by the whole affair at this stage. Why he had two English police officers and a professional bodyguard prancing about in his backyard was, well, almost good fun. The fact that he was doing it without the knowledge or blessing of his superiors added another element to it, a bit like the chilli added to a Putanesca as the final flourish to an already flavoursome dish.

"Letting everyone think we are still after Thumper would be the best way to proceed, I think," Bond had said.

Izzo had not disagreed with him. The sting operation had worked and Izzo had two of Mama Cucciolo's soldiers in the cells. They would not talk, but it did not matter. They would both spend a term in Poggioreale for possession of illegal firearms.

But more than just playing a game with the Black Cat, there was something about the affair that did not seem quite right to the Inspector and he wanted to find out what it was. It did not have the hallmarks of the usual Camorra activity. There was a sophisticated touch to what was going on, which belied their approach of shoot to kill and worry about the consequences later.

He was playing with fire by keeping his superiors in the dark, but he was not worried, and was surprised at that lack of worry. If his part in the release of the Detective Sergeant were ever to come to the attention of his superiors, he would be lucky to escape prison, and that would probably mean death. He would be sent to Poggioreale and a large proportion of that prison's inmates were there because Izzo put them there.

The phone on his desk rang. "Pronto."

"Hey, boss, it's Staff Sergeant Cipolle…"

Izzo interrupted. "I know who you are, Franco, you don't need to remind me each time you call."

"Sorry, boss."

"Go on."

"You remember that spate of Land Rover thefts from the Royal Air Force over at Largo Patria?"

"Sergeant, it was only a couple of weeks ago, of course I remember. Or do you think me old enough to have dementia already?"

"No, sir, not at all, but I think you should get down and see this."

"Down where, Sergeant?"

"I am in the viewing room, sir."

A few minutes later Izzo whistled. The slow-motion digital image was taken from a border security camera, which had been electronically distributed to all concerned agencies. As DIA, Izzo's group received all such communiques. It had been on the morning news that a border guard from the Guardia di Finanza had been killed in a hit-and-run up near Gorizia, but Izzo had thought nothing of it. The local police force would be responsible and if it was connected to organized crime, there would be a DIA officer on the case.

The digital imagery showed the incident in lurid detail. "That's an armoured Land Rover," Izzo was looking at it, but not really believing what he saw.

He could imagine the border guard watching the vehicle approach seeing nothing but lights and shadows. The image clearly showed the officer fire a warning shot into the air before he crouched and fired several shots at the vehicle. As the Land Rover smashed the officer against the bunker wall, it was clearly visible under the border control lights. It had been modified with what looked like plate steel, so it would be impossible to stop without aiming at the tyres. And, at night with headlights blazing, the guard no doubt just aimed in the general direction of the driver's seat. Izzo realized that being a British vehicle, which he deduced to be the case because the eye-slot in the armour was on the wrong side, the driver was the opposite side to where the guard had aimed. The poor man died with no chance.

"Get your jacket, Sergeant, we're going to Largo Patria."

When they arrived at the base, the Royal Air Force Regiment corporal on the gate viewed their identification in short order and lifted the barrier for them to enter. The guard directed them to the police station on the base and gave them the name of the CID detective who was heading up the case.

"Sergeant Bownes?" Izzo asked as he knocked on the open office door. The man looked up from the report he was perusing and nodded. "I am Inspector Izzo, and this is Staff Sergeant Cipolle. Do you have a moment to respond to some demands?"

"I am very busy; can I ask what it is in relation to?"

"Yes of course, we have some information about the theft of air-force Land Rovers that we would like to share." The Sergeant's face practically shone with that information.

"That is good news, come in and sit down," he said as he got up from behind his desk and extended his hand for a shake. "I was looking at the case-file when you knocked." He waved at the document he had been reading.

Izzo and Cipolle sat on the offered seats and the air-force detective returned to the other side of the desk.

"You have information?" he asked.

"Do you have a video player?" Izzo asked. The Detective nodded.

A few minutes later they were watching the same scenes that Izzo and Cipolle had seen about an hour before. The Inspector looked away as the border guard was thrown against the concrete wall of the guardhouse. Once was enough for him. Not that he was in any way squeamish, but he did not see the need to watch the poor man's death more than once.

"I see," Sergeant Bownes said. "I guess you think that is one of my missing vehicles?"

Izzo nodded.

"That will be easy enough to verify. I assume that the vehicle was abandoned somewhere after the incident?"

Izzo looked at Cipolle. He had been so keen to get to the Royal Air Force base that he had not even considered whether the Land Rover had been abandoned. "It was abandoned in Gorizia, a short distance from the scene of the crime."

"I reckon it would have been sprayed while they were upgrading it to a tank," the Englishman said. "Our old blue air-force paint should be visible underneath. And of course, unless they had time to file it off, the engine block ID will be another means of identifying the vehicle."

"I have a question," Cipolle said.

"Shoot."

"Would those vehicles be used to carry weapons?"

"Not at all, Sergeant, is it?" Cipolle nodded. "They were communications vehicles, used to transport stuff between here and Capodichino. They were hijacked at gunpoint while running that sort of errand. Had they been carrying weapons, I think the hijackers would have found it a little more difficult. Why do you ask?"

"The SOCOs found traces of gun oil when they carried out their investigation, much like someone had been cleaning weapons in the back."

"Didn't they burn it?" Cipolle looked a little confused until he realized the English police Sergeant was referring to the criminals, and not the SOCOs who had investigated the abandoned vehicle.

"They set charges to destroy the evidence, but the charges did not ignite. We think they were too far away by then and so did not miss the explosion." Cipolle did not add that they had found fingerprints all over the driver side of the vehicle. There had been prints on the steering wheel, on the door handle, and even on the rear-view mirror.

Sergeant Bownes thought it very unlikely that the failure of the charge was accidental. It did not seem feasible that someone could set explosive charges to destroy evidence and then not be aware that the charges had not gone off. He guessed that the Italian police officers would not really think that a plausible scenario, either. No, he thought they were probably hiding something from him, but he did not mind. It was none of his business, anyway. When they arrived saying they had information about his missing Land Rovers, he thought they were going to say they had found one or both, not that they had been used in the murder of a border guard. Well, he supposed in a sense they had found one of the vehicles and that meant half his case file could be effectively closed.

"Okay, Inspector, so what do you need from me?"

"The men who were hijacked, did they see the hijackers?"

"Yes, it was as if they didn't care whether they would be caught. I sent identikit drawings to the Carabineer Lieutenant responsible for the case. The main thing is, though, there were two of them. They were armed with pistols and wearing Chicago White Sox baseball caps."

Izzo looked at Cipolle then. The Sergeant could see the anger smouldering behind the eyes of his boss. There would be hell to pay if the Black Cats had caused a delay in the investigation because of their immaturity when it came to inter-departmental collaboration.

"Can you give me copies, please. And the serial numbers of the Land Rover engines?"

Sergeant Bownes nodded and left the room. He returned a few minutes later with the requested items. Izzo thanked him profusely and they left.

"I'm very sorry, Franco," Izzo said in the car on the way back to Pozzuoli. "When I saw the images this morning I was so excited I just rushed headlong into the investigation without asking you if you had any information."

Cipolle laughed and winked, "Yes, I know. It's not often I can get one over on the boss."

Chapter 23

Detective Sergeant Standing was sitting on a metal bench outside a bar a few doors up from the restaurant in Posillipo. He had a clear view of the awning and the street tables where some diners were enjoying a leisurely lunch. He wore mirror sunglasses and a hat, so that he would not be recognized on the off chance one of the guys they had nicknamed White Sox One and Two might pass. To anyone who took the time to look at him, Standing looked like an off-duty sailor enjoying the view of the Bay of Naples with a bottle of Peroni and the air of one who had already consumed too many.

He had the mobile phone numbers of Moses, Thumper and Izzo on speed dial, although only Thumper was in the vicinity. Izzo was in the police station monitoring activity and Moses was sleeping in the hotel in Castellammare di Stabia, because he had had the late shift and sat in the hotel room all night staring through the half-closed venetian Blinds at the rear entrance to the restaurant. In fairness, he did volunteer for the shift. Apparently, as a bodyguard he was used to sleepless nights. Besides, he said he would use the time to study the mugshot file. All three of them had been given a copy of the file that contained pictures of the mafia soldiers who belonged to the Cucciolo family. Izzo had asked Sergeant Cipolle to give them the file so they could distinguish the Mafia soldiers from restaurant punters.

There were only two means of access into the restaurant, and Thumper had the rear covered from the seedy hotel. Archie had booked the room and paid a week in advance when Thumper was in the nick. He supposed that any illicit comings and goings would happen through the back door and not the front.

After Thumper's release and the foiled attempt on his and Archie's lives, the four of them met in the bar in Castellammare di Stabia to decide what they would do going forward. Although their goals were slightly different, Izzo needing to resolve the double homicide on Nisida and the death of a border guard, Archie and Thumper needing to save Alliss Junior and Standing needing to resolve the murder of Alliss Senior, they realized that the targets of their investigations were probably the same, namely the Cucciolo crime family.

They had agreed that keeping La Orchidea under observation was pretty much the only course of action. Izzo himself could not afford the resources to keep the place under surveillance, because despite evidence that the Alliss boy was connected to the murders on Nisida, and the connection between him and the Cucciolo family, Izzo's superiors wanted him to concentrate on the recent events in the north and the connection with the Land Rover thefts from Largo Patria. Izzo understood. The death of a Guardia di Finanza officer would always take precedence over the death of two known Camorriste in what appeared to be little more than an inter-family squabble. Despite the creation of the DIA, some things would never change. On this occasion, though, Izzo agreed with the orders he had been given. If they let the murder of the officer go unpunished, it could lead to a form of anarchy that was best avoided. He also needed to be careful, because he was already breaking several regulations and could be in serious trouble if his activities were discovered by his superiors.

Standing tried not to look too interested when he saw White Sox One walk in through the front door of the restaurant. The man still looked out of place with himself, never mind his surroundings. He was wearing the same Armani light summer suit and Ray-Ban sunglasses he had worn in the airport. The DS could not see from this distance, but knew that the man would also be wearing the same patent leather shoes.

Standing speed dialled Thumper. "Heads up, something is in the offing."

Dick Thumper did not respond, but disconnected and concentrated on the back door of the restaurant. It was only a few minutes later when a man wearing a baseball cap walked out with the Camorrista Ricci Tognolli, the man who had taken Chris Alliss to the meeting in Pompeii. He knew his name was Ricci Tognolli thanks to the mugshot file. Tognolli was a senior soldier in the Cucciolo family who had served two terms in Poggioreale for shooting incidents and was suspected of several syndicate-related homicides.

As Tognolli and White Sox One climbed into a car, Thumper speed dialled Standing.

"Red Alpha Romeo, heading up Petrarca."

"Okay. Keep the line open and your headphones in. We have to work in tandem if we're going to pull this off."

"Will do." Thumper said, before running down the stairs and climbing into the unmarked car Izzo had provided. Somehow, they all agreed that the pink Fiat 500 with a British registration would stand out in an undercover operation, as would Archie's hire car with Dutch plates. Izzo had a fleet of rusty second-hand cars, which were little more than bangers, full of the dents and scratches that acted as camouflage in a city like Naples, where dent-free cars were uncommon. Izzo had provided each of the three with one of the cars.

The Alpha Romeo stayed on the backstreets as it drove through the city, keeping to the speed limit. Not the limit imposed by the highway code, but the limit that seemed to be the consensus of all the drivers in the area as they ignored road signs and whipped in and out of the dense traffic, which struck Thumper like some sort of Flamingo mating ritual. They would only have been conspicuous if they had stayed within the legal speed limit.

Standing and Thumper took it in turns to lead the tail, so that neither car would be visible to the occupants of the Alpha for too long. Thumper was not experienced in tailing suspects, so followed the instructions that Standing constantly gave him through their open phone lines. It seemed to work, when about an hour after leaving the restaurant, the Alpha pulled up outside a walled villa and the guy in Ray-Bans climbed out and unlocked the gate.

"What do we do now?" Thumper asked after the red car had driven into the compound.

"We wait. Call Moses, will you?"

An hour and a half later, Thumper heard a knock on the car roof and Archie opened the door and climbed in beside him.

"Did ya find me okay?"

"Naw, I'm still lost in the one-way system," Archie laughed.

"Okay, very funny."

"What's going on?"

"We tailed Tognolli here with White Sox One. They're in that compound over there with the grey steel gate."

"Any sign of Alliss?"

"No, none. But then I can't see over the wall. I did a recce around the place, and this is the only way out. Walled all around. They've got it done up like a fortress."

"Okay, so what does DS Standing think we should do now?" Thumper heard an edge of sarcasm in Archie's voice.

"You know he's a good bloke, right? Me and Adam joined spec ops together. I would trust him with my life."

"Yeah, you might have to. So, where is superman now, by the way?"

"He's gone for some supplies. He saw a supermarket back some ways as we were tailing an Alpha. Says we should keep the front gate under eyeballs until he gets back."

"Who made him the boss?" Archie asked.

"He's from SO7, serious and organized crime. He has a lot of experience with this sort of thing. It's why the brass chose him." Thumper left out that he had also been chosen because of the call that GCHQ had intercepted about the involvement of the Red Brigade. He thought Moses had had enough surprises for the time being, without telling him that they might be hot on the trail of a vicious terrorist organization.

"Yeah, well, forgive me if I don't share your faith with those who command, will you?"

"What the hell got up your arse so sudden?"

"Come on, Dick, you must admit your bosses have treated me pretty shabbily."

"Okay, I admit the bosses have been out of line, but you did break me fuckin' leg, or had you forgotten?"

Archie frowned a little. He guessed his bad mood was due to lack of sleep. The death of his client was not helping, either. He wanted so much to save the boy Alliss, as amends to the father. Not that he was in any way responsible for the death of Alliss Senior, at least he did not think so. He supposed it might be possible that blundering into the meeting in Pompeii might have precipitated the murder in some way, but interrupting the meeting had been at the behest of the lawyer, so was not Archie's fault.

"Sorry, Dick," he said. "Feeling a little rundown at the mo'."

"Yeah, you 'n me both. It's been a long few days."

There was a knock on the roof then and Standing leant down beside the open passenger-side window. "I spoke to Izzo. He asked if we can keep tabs on this place. He thinks the boy is probably in there, but he doesn't want us to act until we know for sure." The pair in the car nodded.

"Is he sending some cops to help?" Archie asked.

"No. All his guys are tied up looking for the arseholes who killed a border-control officer up north.

Apparently, this area is big-time bandit country, so we need to keep switching cars and positions and keep our heads down so no one spots us. S'gonna be a long night, boys." Standing slapped the car roof and walked back to the side street where his own car was parked.

"Okay, I'm going to get some shuteye. You take the first watch, will you?" Archie asked. Thumper nodded and braced himself for a long night of looking over his shoulder.

It was very early the next morning when the grey steel gate swung open and what looked like a military vehicle drove out. Thumper had agreed to take the early morning watch, so he saw the gate open. He could not see who was driving, because the sun had not crested the surrounding buildings and the interior was all shadows. He did see a man in RAF uniform climb out of the back and lock the gate, though. There was something vaguely familiar about the man, but he could not pinpoint it in the early morning half-light. He hit speed dial and asked Archie, "You getting this?" Archie's car was parked in a different side street and he should have been asleep, but he answered the phone so quickly, Thumper guessed he was awake.

"Yeah, I'll take the Land Rover, you stay here and keep watch on the fortress."

"Okay. I'll call Standing."

It was a couple of hours later when the passenger door opened and Archie slipped into the seat beside Dick. "Anything happening?"

"No. What about the Land Rover?"

"I followed it to a NATO base called Bagnoli. Couldn't get on the base, though. My guess is there is also more than one way out, so rather than hang around there, I came back. What's Standing up to?"

"He's got the back wall under surveillance."

Although it was true, Standing was on the corner looking at the back wall of the villa, he was concentrating on a mobile phone call with Inspector Izzo.

"What are you saying to me?" Izzo asked.

"A call was intercepted between someone claiming that they would send the Red Brigade their best soldier, and they named Chris Alliss." The DS had decided to tell Izzo of the possible red Brigade involvement after Dick told him that what seemed to be a British military vehicle had left the compound in the early morning. It seemed a little incongruous for a Mafia gang to be driving a military vehicle, and he was suspicious.

"Where did this call come from?" Izzo asked.

"There are listening stations all over the place. There is even one here in Naples. One of the reasons why the senior brass sent me, is because of that call. AC Bond and Commander Blythe, my boss, knew that Moses was chasing Alliss, so they sent me."

"I thought the Red Brigade was destroyed in the eighties."

"Yes, but now they are back and apparently up to no good."

"So, what do you propose we do?"

"I think we should act now. We have this villa under surveillance, but we could sit here for a month and see nothing. Why don't we just assume that Alliss is in there and go fish him out."

"And what if he is not there? We have seen Tognolli and one man with a baseball cap who followed you in Luton, but we don't know of any crimes they have committed. I am bound by rules, Sergeant."

"You are, Inspector, but we are not. Not really."

"What are you saying to me?"

"Moses is a civilian. Thumper is officially suspended and I am here incognito. If we break into that compound and find nothing, you can blame it on us and not have to face any consequences."

Izzo thought about that. He supposed that in some ways it was true, but what Standing failed to realize was that the Inspector had already broken several rules since this affair started and if they did break into the compound and Alliss was not there, questions would be asked.

"I will call you back, Adam," he said, before hanging up the telephone and opening a new box of paperclips.

Chapter 24

Chris had no idea why he was behind the steering wheel of a Royal Air Force Land Rover at the back of a queue of vehicles waiting to enter the NATO base at Bagnoli. Just as he had been unaware of why the man in the baseball cap behind him in the other modified Land Rover had forced him at gunpoint to break the barrier at the border crossing between Italy and Slovenia, killing a uniformed man in the process. He was scared to the point of nausea of being discovered and arrested for that murder, but not as scared as he was of the man who had taken a picture of his father with his throat in his lap sitting at the table in the Kensington apartment kitchen.

He knew why he was dressed in an RAF uniform, though. For some reason, the men in the back of the Land Rover needed him so they could gain access to the base, which apparently was headquarters for something called AFSOUTH. He guessed they needed him to get them through the barrier because they were probably persons of interest and their English was not good enough. They would have aroused immediate suspicion if asked any questions at all by the guards on the gate.

The nameless men were no longer in their baseball caps, but were sitting in the back of the Land Rover wearing RAF uniforms. One of the men had his feet resting on a tarpaulin, which covered the metal plates they had loaded before leaving the villa in Afragola. There was also something with more bulk under the tarp, but Chris did not want to consider what that might be.

The plates were the same as those they had mounted on the other Land Rover, the one Chris had used to kill the man at the border crossing. Because of that, he knew that these men intended to make the Land Rover into the same sort of armoured vehicle they had used to crash the border. He had no idea why, but knew that it could not be for anything good.

There were two black and red Alpha Romeos parked at the side of the road where they were queueing. Chris could see men in black peaked caps sitting in the cars, watching the queue with intensity. He guessed they were Italian military police, but could see no opportunity to get their attention.

The gate was guarded by US Marines, and Alliss was frantically trying to think of some way to warn them of the impending attack. As they edged forward in what would have appeared to onlookers like a regular RAF vehicle, Alliss studied the guards. Some of them were armed with automatic rifles, and others were using mirrors to check under each vehicle for bombs, but they all looked professional. He peeked up at the rear-view mirror. The man who scared him the most, the one with dead eyes, smiled at him and winked. The wink looked as menacing as one he had seen from a komodo dragon at Regents Park Zoo when he was a kid. He shivered and thought about what Ricci said to him when they were loading the vehicle earlier in the morning. "These two are mad. See what they did to your father. That is nothing to what they will do to you!"

Chris knew it was a threat to keep him compliant, but he also knew it to be true. The day when Chris met the man in Pompeii, he had not paid much attention, not until a gunshot knocked his Ray-Bans off and he saw the eyes. Memory of those eyes was what drove him to follow instructions to the letter. Well, those eyes and the image of a man tied to a chair with his throat cut. A man who Chris was now loath to call father, not because of the way the dead man had betrayed him and his mother, but because doing so would admit that Chris was responsible for his brutal murder. He had wanted Philip Alliss to pay for the betrayal, but not that way.

As the Marine checked his fake ID, Chris gripped the steering wheel until his knuckles whitened and stared at him willing him to sense that there was something wrong. He was about to scream out a warning when he felt something hard nudge him in the small of his back. He knew that it would be a big silver American gun, like the one he had seen 'scary eyes' pull in Pompeii, so he bit his lip and swallowed whatever he was thinking about saying.

The guard gave a cursory look at the fake IDs of the two men in the back, while another glanced over the tailgate and gave a thumbs-up. He turned to the barrier and nodded for the Private First Class to lift the bar. As he drove the Land Rover onto the NATO base, Alliss wondered why they concentrated on the outside of the vehicle and gave the inside only a cursory inspection. He guessed it was probably because the three men in the Land Rover were apparently their allies and their IDs appeared to be in order. It was also a relatively long time since the last conflict ended, so their vigilance might be affected by that tranquillity.

After they were through the barrier, 'scary eyes' directed him to drive behind what appeared to be a hangar and told him to get out. Chris climbed down and looked around the dusty base. He had his eyes to the front and so did not see as 'scary eyes' approached and smacked him on the back of the head with the heavy Smith and Wesson he favoured.

Admiral Oswald Benbow was proud of his command. For a tearaway Afro-American from Queens in New York to have gained the rank of admiral was already an achievement in "This Man's Navy", but to receive the command of Allied Forces Southern Europe (AFSOUTH), one of the most strategic commands in NATO, could only be considered remarkable. He liked to think he did not allow the appointment to inflate his ego and that he was a fair commander. He believed that he listened to the advice of his subordinates, and treated the inferior allied forces under his command with the respect they deserved. During the Gulf War, Benbow had been an instrumental player on the staff of 'Stormin'

Norman Schwarzkopf and it was recognition for the part he played in the invasion of Kuwait and its aftermath that saw him promoted to the rank of Allied Commander, AFSOUTH.

The admiral was sitting in his large affluent office reading a report about how the ranks were selling their cigarette rations to local Mafiosi, when a commotion in the front office caused him to look up from a list of proposals about how to combat the black marketeering. He heard what appeared to be a muffled shot and a thump, like something heavy hitting the floor.

"Davison!" he shouted through the closed door. There was no response. It was not like Lieutenant Davison to ignore the admiral. He flipped the intercom switch up and repeated, "Davison," still no response. Something was wrong.

Benbow picked up the telephone to call his security officer, Lieutenant Ricks, when his office door crashed open and two armed and masked men ran in, pointing what appeared to be heavy calibre pistols at his head.

"What is the meaning of this?" The admiral protested, as he was hauled to his feet and his mouth and nose were covered by a cloth with a sweet cloying smell. Benbow gagged and fought for breath. Chloroform, he thought, as he lost consciousness.

Private First Class Rudy Rotenase was looking at the black and red Alpha Romeos parked at the side of the road a little down from the barrier onto the base. Not for the first time he was wondering why the Italian Military Police felt they needed a presence outside the base. It could be construed as an insult to the Marines, like they were incapable of guarding their own bases, or something. He looked over at the gunny, who had taken over checking the IDs of those queueing to get through the barrier. They were a good team, him and the gunny. Each time he nodded, Rudy would lift the barrier and wave the vehicle through. Gunnery Sergeant Kerplunski had said they were insecure and needed to feel they were part of everything.

PFC Rotenase heard a screeching of tyres coming from the rear and spun around to see what looked like an armoured car bearing down on the barrier at speed. He looked at gunny to see what to do and followed the lead of bringing his automatic rifle off his shoulder. Gunny pointed his weapon above the vehicle and fired a warning shot. If anything, rather than slowing down, they picked up speed. Rotenase only had time for one small burst of his weapon before he had to leap aside and let the armoured vehicle crash through the barrier. No one had a chance to raise the tank traps or get off more than a sporadic burst of gunfire before the vehicle was through the gate.

Rotenase looked up from his position on the tarmac to see the two red and black Alpha Romeos shredded by heavy calibre machine gun fire and the armoured vehicle swing around the corner of the crossroads that led away from the base.

Admiral Benbow awoke with his left wrist chained to a metal cot in what appeared to be a cellar. He guessed he was underground because of the elevated window and the greyness of the light that filtered through the frosted glass. His head was thumping, probably a side effect of the chloroform they administered when they kidnapped him. He thought briefly about shouting for help, before realizing it would be a futile gesture. He did not doubt that whoever kidnapped him would have considered the eventuality of rescue and if shouting would help, they would have gagged him. He was vaguely thankful that they had not and that he could breathe easily. He tested his bonds and found that he could move quite freely, to the extent that he could sit up and get a better look at the room. As he did so, he realized that he was in his shorts and tee-shirt and his feet were bare.

He was looking around the small space when he heard the key turn in the lock. The door opened to admit two men carrying a third between them. The third man was in British RAF uniform. From the loll of the serviceman's head, the admiral could tell he was unconscious, or worse.

"What is the meaning of this?" he asked, more to get a feel for his captors than because he expected them to answer. The two men ignored him and threw the man in uniform onto the floor in the corner of the room. Before they left, they did not bother to undress the man and chain him to a cot, so the admiral guessed his fate had already been sealed. However, there was no sign of blood, so Benbow hoped they had overdone the chloroform and the RAF serviceman would come to presently.

"Can you hear me?" he called, attempting to wake him up. There was no response. Benbow prayed fervently that the man would recover. The thought of spending who knew how long with nothing but a corpse for company was not very appealing. It was also the height of summer and he imagined that a dead body in this space would quickly become very ripe.

And then he thought about the two men who had carried him in. They were not young men and both had sawn-off shotguns slung over their shoulders, which the admiral knew were called lupara. But more importantly, neither of them had worn a mask. Not wearing a mask when in front of the man you had kidnapped, could only mean one thing, the admiral thought. Although it might be different in Italy, he supposed. He knew that kidnapping here was much more commonplace than in the United States. He hoped it was different in Italy, and that kidnappers were so untouchable that they did not need to bother disguising themselves.

"Can you hear me?" he tried again, but there was still no response. I wonder how long he will take to start stinking the place out, the admiral thought.

"What are we going to do now?" Archie asked.

They had seen the armoured car drive in through the grey metal gates. When it left earlier in the morning it had been an ordinary British military vehicle, maybe a Land Rover. Admittedly when it drove out of the compound it was veiled by the early morning light, but still recognizable as an off-road vehicle. When it returned, it had plate metal sheets bolted to it and an eye-slit on the right-hand side of the plate that covered the windscreen. It also appeared to be marked with what looked very much like bullet dents.

"I guess we call Adam and ask him."

"Look, Dick, we know something is going on. I saw that Land Rover drive onto a military base this morning. Now we see it back here made up like a tank with bullet holes in it. We need to do something!"

"I agree, we need to do something, but let's wait until Adam gets here. We can discuss how best to proceed when we're all together. Why don't *you* call him?" Thumper asked, trying to bridge the gap that was developing between them. Moses shrugged and was about to call when the back door opened and Standing slid into the passenger seat.

"Anything happening?"

Chapter 25

Inspector Izzo stood in Admiral Benbow's office and looked around at the lavish furnishings. The office space was dominated by a large oak desk with a brass fitted lamp in the form of an eagle. Most of the top was occupied with a red leather cover. A folder with pages marked secret lay open, which Izzo supposed the admiral had been reading when he was abducted. The only other evidence of the kidnapping was the chair behind the desk lying on its side and the body of the naval officer in the reception area. The man had a black hole in his forehead and nothing where the back of his skull used to be. If not for that and the broken barrier down by the main gate, Izzo doubted anyone would even know the admiral had been kidnapped.

"No one heard anything?" he asked.

"No, it would seem they used a silencer."

Izzo wrung his hands in frustration. He desperately needed a Gauloise, but the Americans would not let anyone smoke in the admiral's office. Apparently, the admiral was a staunch non-smoker and they were not about to let someone contaminate his personal space for when he returned.

"Any thoughts?" Sergeant Bownes asked.

"There is not much to see here, Sergeant," Izzo shrugged.

He was surprised to even be in the office and more surprised that the secret document in the middle of the desk had not been removed. The American military were not normally open to interference from local police agencies when it came to internal police matters, that is, crimes that were committed on NATO and US military bases. However, he guessed they realized that on this occasion they were out of their depth. The audacity of this raid onto a military base had each of the investigators in awe. To attack a base full of armed personnel in the middle of the day and then break through the barrier in what was, in essence, a tank, showed not only a high-level of planning, but also a courage that, had they not kidnapped a senior US navy officer, would be admired.

From what Izzo understood, Sergeant Bownes had been called because one of the missing Land Rovers was used in the attack. Bownes was known to be investigating the hijacked military vehicles. On top of that, the CCTV footage from the base entrance showed that the vehicle had RAF markings and that the driver appeared to be an RAF serviceman, so etiquette dictated that the RAF police should be involved in any ongoing investigation.

The Marines who allowed the vehicle access to the base could not recall anything specific about the Land Rover, or the driver. They screened several hundred vehicles every day and would only remember those that had seemed out of place for whatever reason. The investigators could only surmise from that information that the Land Rover had been ordinary when it was allowed access.

Several Marines fired at the Land Rover as it left the base, but had been unable to stop it. On hindsight, they knew they should have aimed at the tyres, but the heat of the moment prevented them from reaching that conclusion as the Land Rover crashed the barrier and raced away down the access road to the base. The two Carabineer cars that were always parked at the main entrance were sprayed with heavy calibre automatic fire from the back of the vehicle as it drove past their position, so they were unable to give chase. By the time the alarm had been raised, the armoured car was long gone and the law enforcement agencies knew there was little or no point in asking for witnesses.

It was Sergeant Bownes who suggested calling in Izzo, because he was the DIA Inspector for the region and already involved in the case of the missing Land Rovers. Bownes suggested that the kidnappers were Mafia had argued that the Italian would provide invaluable insights into their way of thinking. The NCIS Senior Field Agent in charge of the investigation, had surprisingly agreed.

"They used the Land Rover to break the barrier, as they did in the North?" The Italian asked. Bownes nodded. "So it would seem that the border crashing in Gorizia was a dress practice?"

"A dress rehearsal," Bownes corrected. "Yes, that would be my guess."

"What do you mean, a dress rehearsal?" SFA Wendy Haus, asked.

"Someone killed a Guardia on the border with Slovenia." Bownes answered her. "There was apparently no motive for the killing. Inspector Izzo now thinks it was probably a rehearsal for this kidnapping." The SFA nodded her understanding.

"But I think it was more than just a dress practice," Izzo continued his thought process aloud. "There were the prints of fingers all over the Land Rover we recovered in Gorizia. I am thinking that something devious is going on."

"Devious how?" SFA Haus asked.

"There were explosives in the car, that did not explode. I think that someone is planning for blame to be placed where it does not belong."

"So, Inspector, you think our cases are connected?"

"Yes, most definitely connected. No one saw anything?"

"No. There is CCTV footage of the arrival. It appeared to be driven by an RAF corporal on the way in." The SFA looked pointedly at Bownes then, as if he was responsible. "When the vehicle broke out, no one could see through the armour, so there was no way of knowing if it was driven by the same person."

"Can I see the video?" Izzo asked. Bownes nodded and the SFA took them both into the next room where she had a projector already set up.

Two minutes later Izzo was chewing on a toothpick and wondering what he should say to the two investigators frowning up at him expectantly. Or more accurately, how he should say it. The driver of the Land Rover on the way into Bagnoli NATO base was Christopher Alliss. His face was clearly visible and he was not wearing a hat, or gloves for that matter. Izzo could read tension in the way he gripped the steering wheel and stared intently at the

Marine Gunnery Sergeant, as if willing him to act. There was a plea there for all to see, if only they knew to look.

The Inspector's mind was working frantically to try and piece together the individual elements of the puzzle and reach a solution. The plot to kidnap a senior American naval officer must have taken a good deal of planning. Alliss had only been in the country for what, about a month? He had been mentioned by someone suspected of being a high-ranking syndicate member in an intercepted telephone conversation, which Izzo had only heard about earlier in the day from DS Standing.

"Have there been any money demands?" he asked.

"Not yet."

Izzo frowned. The Camorra would not be averse to a little kidnapping to make money. It was never their main source of income, but they had been known on occasion to sanction it when in need of an injection of capital. For them to kidnap a senior NATO officer was unheard of, unless they were working with someone else. Now seemingly, they were working with the Red Brigade, an organization he had thought no longer existed, until the English detective told him about the intercepted conversation. Izzo seemed to recall that prior to their falling out in the early eighties, the Camorra had been known to assist the BR in high profile kidnappings. It had been when the BR kidnapped a well-known and liked politician that the Camorra decided to assist law enforcement agencies in bringing them to justice. Surely, after that rift, the BR and the Camorra would no longer be keen on getting into bed together?

The crackdown in the eighties had seen all the Red Brigade's senior members either killed or captured and that could be laid squarely at the feet of the Camorra, or more specifically at the feet of Papa Cucciolo, Izzo remembered with a start. The BR had then exacted reprisals against the syndicates by indiscriminately killing any members they could get at. No, Izzo could not see them getting back into bed together. His chain of thought was interrupted by the ringing of his mobile phone. He shrugged an apology at Bownes and Haus before retreating from the office to take the call.

"Izzo."

"Inspector, Standing. We need to talk."

"I am very occupied now, Adam. We must talk later."

Izzo was about to press the end call button when Standing emphasized the urgency, "It is directly related to the kidnapping of Christopher Alliss." Izzo frowned. At this moment, he did not care about Christopher Alliss. The kidnapping of the admiral was much more important.

"An RAF Land Rover left the villa compound this morning and Archie followed it to somewhere called Bagnoli, AFSOUTH. A few moments ago, it got back here full of bullet holes."

Izzo looked over his shoulder to make sure that the two military investigators were not listening to the conversation. He needed time to weigh up his options before he included a wider audience.

"Did you see who was driving?" he asked. Not that he really cared who was driving. He was speaking to allow himself time to assimilate what he had just heard. A Land Rover had left the compound in the morning and returned armoured. That meant the admiral was in Afragola. But what was he to do with that information?

"No, there was a metal shield across the windscreen, with what looked remarkably like bullet holes in it. The gate was closed before anyone got out of the vehicle, so we saw nothing of interest."

"Okay, Adam, I will call you back soon. For now, do nothing."

The inspector walked back into the admiral's office.

"I am sorry," he said. "I have been called away by my boss. I must return to Pozzuoli."

The two detectives did not hide their bemusement as they watched the dapper Italian walk away from the investigation. He had been next to useless during the short period in the Admiral's office.

"You thought he would be of use, why?" Haus asked the bemused Bownes, who shrugged.

Izzo sat in his car for several minutes before starting the engine. His suspicions had been growing more pronounced as the events of the day unfolded. The knowledge that the Cucciolo family were somehow involved in the kidnapping of the admiral was worrying him. He could see that the Red Brigade would benefit from kidnapping a highly political figure, but why the Camorra. When he cast his mind back to the events of the early nineteen-eighties and the involvement of Papa Cucciolo, he could not believe that the two were working together. It just did not add up.

Izzo was a suspicious man by nature and the more the events began to unfurl the more he suspected something other than just Camorra involvement. And the Red Brigade, where had they been for the last sixteen years? No, creating a successful terrorist organization took time and resources, time and resources that the New Red Brigade would probably not have. The Cucciolo family would have those resources, but who would have put the two disparate elements together?

He started the car and drove towards the exit. A US Marine saw him coming and lifted the temporary barrier, despite the additional security. As Izzo drove off the base, he saw that two additional cars were parked beside the bullet-ridden Alphas, which had been shot up during the admiral's kidnapping. The Black Cats had their own checkpoint in place outside the base. As he neared the cars, an officer flagged him down.

"Inspector Izzo?" he asked as Pietro pulled up beside him.

"Yes, how can I help you, Captain?"

"Please leave your vehicle and come with me."

"What is the meaning of this?" Izzo asked as the officer opened his door and beckoned him out of the car.

"You are under arrest, Inspector, for obstructing an ongoing investigation and attempting to divert the course of justice."

"You cannot do this," Izzo fumed. "What gives you the right?"

"I am a Captain in the Carabineers. If I think that a police officer is obstructing an ongoing investigation, I have every right to arrest him."

Izzo did not believe his ears, as the captain opened the back door of his black and red Alpha Romeo and protected the inspector's head as he forced him in.

Chapter 26

They were sitting in the dented unmarked car that Thumper was using, trying to decide what course of action to take when the heavy metal gate opened and a big Italian trial bike exited, ridden by two men in Armani suits, Ray-Bans and Chicago White Sox baseball caps.

"Knee length One and Two together. Not seen that before," Standing mused.

"Knee length?" Thumper asked.

"Knee length White Sox."

"Ah, very clever."

"They're not wearing any helmets," Archie said.

"Yeah, bit lax around here with the helmet laws," Thumper agreed.

"You'd think the way they drive they'd wear helmets to bed," Archie laughed.

They had been sitting outside the compound for most of the day and sunset was arriving. There had been no word from Izzo, and they were beginning to lose patience.

"Now's our chance," Adam said. "Two of them gone, that can't leave many. And my guess is those two are the pros of the group."

"What makes you say that?" Archie asked.

"With my training, I can spot a pro a mile away."

"Seriously, we don't know how many are in there." Thumper did not want them making any mistakes through over-enthusiasm. They did not even know if Alliss was in there.

"We've been watching the place for what, best part of two days," Archie said. "We've seen Tognolli and White Sox One and Two go in. God knows how many come out and go back in in the Land Rover, then the Knee Highs ride out. That's not a lot of activity over a twenty-four-hour period. I reckon Adam is right, not many in there."

"Yeah, whatever the hell is going on, I'm thinking there's a skeleton crew inside," Standing iterated.

"How'll we get in?" asked Thumper.

"We climb the wall."

"There's broken glass cemented into the top."

"We can use the car carpets to cover the glass as we go over. You know, old special forces style."

"What is it with you and special forces?" Thumper asked. "You tried out for the SAS and they rejected you. Build a bridge and get over it!"

Standing frowned. He had not wanted Archie to know that he too had been rejected by the Regiment. It had also been the reason why he left the army, although not in the same way that

Archie had. Standing took voluntary retirement when there was a promotion to move some military servicemen into the police service, because of a perceived shortage of officers in The Met and a glut of soldiers.

"You are sure this is the best course of action?" Archie asked Standing.

"We can't reach Izzo. I don't know what has got into him. When I phoned just now his phone went straight to some sort of messaging service. He was okay when I phoned earlier."

"What did he say, exactly?" Thumper asked.

"He told me that he would get back to me. He should have called by now."

"Okay, do we really want to do this without Izzo's say-so?"

"We won't have a better opportunity in my book."

Thumper looked at Archie, who nodded.

"The back alley is really shady, and night is just around the corner" Standing said, "so I think we just go over the back wall, one at a time. First over keeps an eye out on the inside. Last over keeps an eye out on the outside."

They agreed the order in which they would go over the wall. Each of them checked their pistol, a habit for those trained in the use of firearms, and made their way down the quickly darkening back alley. First over the wall was Archie. He landed without noise in the dust of a back-garden space badly in need of some care and attention. He could tell that this area of the villa never saw sunlight. The shadows were deep and menacing. He crouched against the wall, guessing he would be invisible from the interior of the villa.

"Archie?" Dick whispered from on top of the wall.

"Here, against the wall. Make sure you don't land on me." Archie heard a muffled thump and saw Thumper sprawled in the dust a few feet away.

"See anything?" he asked.

"No, all is quiet. I reckon they are keeping eyes on the gate. Probably not expecting trouble, either, seeing as we are smack in the middle of bandit country."

They both watched as Standing landed in the dust in a feline crouch, looking like a tiger about to pounce. Archie shook his head and smiled. "You been practicing?"

Standing looked over his shoulder and frowned, "What?"

"Never mind. How do you want to do this?"

"You two go to the left and I will go to the right. Keep your backs to the wall so anyone looking out can't see you."

"What about any cellar windows?" Thumper asked, pointing to under the veranda at the back of the villa where anyone looking out of would see their legs passing.

"It's almost pitch black out here. The only way we will be seen is if someone opens the shutters and light comes from the inside."

Archie and Thumper conceded the point. They all ran to the wall in a crouch and began to edge around the building, as Standing had suggested. Archie could not believe the tension he felt as he crept along the wall with the pistol he had taken from Pompeii in one hand and the other resting against the paintwork on the side of the villa so he could feel his way along. He could sense Thumper creeping along behind him, but dared not take his eyes from the front in case someone should walk around the other corner of the building. Everything seemed extremely quiet, as if the town was holding its breath waiting for events in the villa to explode. As Archie neared the front corner of the house he could feel his heart beating in his chest. To him, it seemed loud enough for someone in the villa to hear. When he reached the corner, he got down on his hands and knees and chanced a quick look around the corner at ground level, thinking that whoever was guarding would be looking at head height and not down at ankle height.

There were spotlights on the front of the villa, illuminating the space between the gate and the veranda, so he could see an old man sitting on a white plastic chair with a shotgun on his lap. The man was staring fixedly at the gate, not bothering with the sides of the house. It's so difficult to get good goons these days, flashed through Archie's mind, and he almost laughed. He leant backwards and whispered to Dick that there was a single man on the balcony with a shotgun. It was as he was turning back towards the front that he felt something hard and metallic press against his left cheek. He turned his eyes to the left, not daring to move his head, and saw the silhouette of a man with a balaclava pressing a gun to his cheek and holding his finger in front of his hood at mouth height.

"Shush," Archie just heard.

Seconds later the main gate to the compound crashed open and an armoured personnel carrier burst into the space before the house. He heard a couple of gunshots and the man in the white plastic chair was dead before the APC came to a stop. Archie watched as armed men wearing balaclavas swarmed from the vehicle and broke down the front door to burst into the villa.

After that, everything happened extremely fast. The man kept his gun pressed to Archie's cheek for a few minutes during which time Archie heard several gunshots and lots of shouted conversation in Italian. He could not move his head and so had no idea how Thumper was faring. After the noise of what he assumed was the last gunshot died down, his captor pushed him in the small of the back with his gun and said, "Move."

Archie moved to the front of the villa. Standing was kneeling in the dust with his hands interlocked behind his head and a furious look on his face. Archie was told to kneel beside Standing and interlock his own fingers. As he did so, he chanced a glance to his right. Dick was there, with his own guard in a balaclava and his own furious look.

While the three of them were kneeling in the dust with guns pressed to their faces, they watched other men in balaclavas run out of the villa shepherding a podgy, middle-aged Afro-American in his underwear. Archie could see the supine body of the man who had been sitting in a white plastic chair and surmised that there were other bodies in the villa, judging by the number of rounds that had been fired.

No one, apart from their personal guards, paid any attention to the three men kneeling in the dust. The villa was a hive of activity for what seemed like hours before Archie was herded into the back of an army jeep and taken away.

He was locked up in what he assumed to be a military prison and left to rot for three days. He had a TV in his cell and was brought meals three times a day, but nobody spoke to him. He gave up asking to speak to a lawyer after the third meal had been placed in the door slot and the guard who delivered it totally ignored him. It was while eating that meal that he saw on CNN the Italian Secret Service had rescued a certain Admiral Benbow and that four kidnappers had been killed during the rescue, including an Englishman who was the son of a prominent lawyer murdered in London the previous week.

The assumption was that the boy had murdered his father because he had stumbled onto something related to the kidnap plot. That assumption was not confirmed by law enforcement, but neither was it denied.

It was at the end of those three days when Archie was driven to the military air-force base at Capodichino. His captors said nothing as they handed him over to the Italian military police, Carabineers, in their black uniforms. They got him to sign a document that he did not understand before they handed him over to an RAF police Sergeant called Bownes.

"You're lucky," the Sergeant said. "The Italians are washing their hands of you."

"What about the others?" Archie asked.

"Already gone. They were flown out of here the next morning. Gonna be hell to pay for those two."

"And Izzo?"

"Arrested for obstruction of justice. He will be lucky not to get a prison sentence."

Archie was flown to RAF Brize Norton in a C-130 Hercules. There was a Metropolitan Police Service paddy wagon waiting for him on the tarmac, and he was driven to London with a chatty lady police constable driving him spare all the way.

Please, please, please, he had thought, spare me any more of this wittering, as the paddy wagon pulled off the base in Oxfordshire and headed for the M40.

Chapter 27

Mama looked at the Fratelli Sconosciuti with an expression that would curdle milk before it had a chance to leave the cow. These two boys who had never failed her before, had failed her now. All they needed to do was get the New Red Brigade leaders into the room with the admiral and the Alliss boy and then kill them all, nothing so difficult in that, not really.

She looked at them on the other side of the meeting table in the restaurant office. They looked like children sitting outside the headmaster's study waiting to be chastised for stealing the communal wine. Mama shook her head at the injustice of it all. It had been so simple in the planning. Nothing could have prepared them, though, for the bumbling interruptions caused by the arrival of Moses and the giant, blond-haired police officer.

Mama thought back to how the whole episode had begun.

When the Italian Secret Service approached her, she thought that her birthday, her saint's day and Christmas day had all arrived together. They told her that they had an undercover agent in a splinter group of the Red Brigade, the terrorist organization that had caused her family to lose so much face. The new group was called the New Red Brigade. The New Red Brigade were keen to break the law and bomb supermarkets or kidnap the rich, but they did not have the resources. The ISS approached Mama because they needed some help, like they had in the eighties when they approached Papa in Poggioreale. This time they came because Mama had the resources the New Red Brigade needed to give their cause the boost it so desperately wanted.

For the ISS, the task was simple. Their undercover agent would promote the Camorra as a way for the group to reignite their struggle against the capitalist oppressor and then propose the Cucciolo family as the one to carry the torch for them.

Mama had smiled and nodded and been amazed at the poetic bent of the Secret Service higher echelons who dreamt up the plan. The Brigade had no idea that the Cucciolo family was the same family who betrayed them in the early eighties. All they knew was Papa had been the ring leader. Papa to them, was the name of a Capo with power who operated out of Poggioreale, and there was no way they could connect the Cucciolo family with the 'pentito', or state's witness who betrayed them to the authorities when everything went sour. The slaughter they perpetrated in the aftermath of that betrayal had been indiscriminate, perhaps the real reason why the name Papa became an eternal anathema after the fact. The other families might have forgotten over time, if not forgiven, except that his betrayal had cost them so many lives in that bloody slaughter.

As far as the ISS was concerned, it all went to plan until the leadership of the Brigade asked for the death of Papa as a gesture of faith from the family. Of course, they did not know that Papa and Mama were connected. They just surmised that the families would all be party to each other's business and that if anyone could find the location of a pentito, it would be the same people who owned most of the country's law-enforcement senior officers. The ISS had hemmed and hawed and pretended that it was unethical to betray someone in witness protection, before providing Mama with the necessary details. There had been a pang of sadness when Mama sent the boys to Boston to execute their own father, but it was fleeting.

She looked up from her thoughts and asked the boys, "So why were you not in the villa?"

"We went to make the call to the NRB, so they could come to see the admiral and make the ransom demands," Stefano, her eldest, answered.

The way the ISS had planned it, at that point, they would storm the villa and arrest everyone, taking the New Red Brigade leaders into custody, thereby thwarting yet another terrorist action and making international headlines as a leader in the fight against global terrorism. That was not how Mama Cucciolo had envisaged the outcome, however. The Fratelli Sconosciuti were supposed to have a surprise waiting for the ISS when they arrived. When the ISS broke into the compound, the Admiral was to be found dead with the young English boy and the two old guards. They would then place the blame for the kidnapping and death squarely at the feet of the disillusioned Englishman and the Brigade, because the ISS would not be able to announce to the world how they had manipulated the affair to suit their own needs. It would be preferable for the ISS to admit that the American admiral had died in the rescue attempt, than for them to admit that they had instigated the affair. The death of the admiral would no doubt have caused a diplomatic incident, but would not have caused a war.

"Why did you not call from the villa?" Mama broke her reverie. She wanted to find out what had happened in the lead up to her plan failing so dramatically.

"We didn't want the two old farts or Tognolli to overhear," Roberto, the second son, answered. Roberto was younger only by a few minutes and so Mama held him less responsible for the failure.

Mama looked at the two boys who had murdered their father in Boston. Of course, neither son knew that he was their father. They were only babies when he was sent to prison, and Mama could see no reason to tell them that Papa was in Poggioreale. After he turned pentito, the whole family was so ashamed to be associated with Papa, that no one ever mentioned him again and so neither boy had ever heard of him. Whenever they asked after their father, Mama would smile and say, "Long gone, long gone."

She liked to fantasize that the boys believed Papa to be some sort of folk hero who had died in a tragic cause, but knew it to be just that, fantasy. She watched them grow up with more than a passing interest in physical violence and sent them to an expensive boarding school in New York, where she hoped they would learn to be civilized. When they returned as young men, no one knew them and they became known as the Fratelli Sconosciuti. Mama liked that name and all that it encompassed. They were her unknown soldiers and everybody feared them.

It was a small blessing that no one in the family had known of the plan. Their failure would have destroyed the fearsome reputation they commanded.

"The Alliss boy was supposed to be killed in the fusillade of the rescue," she said in a calm voice, which made the twins very nervous. When Mama spoke calmly, she was usually very angry.

"I hit him too hard on the base, he never came to and bled out in the Land Rover," Stefano admitted.

She had expected Stefano as the eldest, to keep his brother to the plan. He was so much harder than Roberto and Mama supposed she was more disappointed in him for that.

"What happened then?"

"When we went back to the villa, after calling the NRB, it was swarming with ISS. For some reason, they attacked early." Mama knew why the ISS had attacked early, because they had told her when she called her handler, furious that her plan had failed.

The Englishmen were about to stumble on the admiral and rescue him purely by accident. There was no way that they would give up all their hard-earned credit, because a couple of English policemen and a suspected criminal had stumbled onto the villa where he was being held. They would miss the real target of the senior Brigade members, but so what? They needed to be seen to rescue the admiral as much as they needed to arrest the New Red Brigade, who were nothing more than a toothless tiger in all honesty.

"One of you is to be punished," she said. "You can decide amongst yourselves who it is, but I need to know by the end of the day."

There was a knock on the office door then. "Come," Mama said.

Francesco opened the door a crack and stuck his head through the gap. "Your visitor has arrived, Mama."

"Thank you, Francesco. Show him in, please. You two can leave and decide who will be punished for your failure. You must tell me before the evening meal."

Fully chastised, the twins left the office. As they made their way through the door, Francesco opened it fully and gestured Mama's guest to enter.

"Ah, Signor Elenco, I am pleased to meet you finally," Mama said as she came around the front of her desk and indicated that he should sit in the admiral's chair at the head of the table.

"I am afraid Detective Sergeant, that the disciplinary board had no choice but to find you guilty of gross misconduct," Assistant Commissioner Bond said with a look of pity mixed with sorrow, which Dick Thumper knew to be as sincere as when Nixon claimed no knowledge of Watergate. Gross misconduct carried only one punishment, dismissal from the Service. Bond was sitting on the other side of the meeting table in his office with Commander

Willett, Chief Superintendent Rogers-Smythe and Superintendent Douglas. The Supers were both looking at the wall a few inches above Thumper's head and would not meet his steady gaze.

Thumper stood at attention in his dress uniform and thought about how he would fight this unfair dismissal. He did not believe that his superiors could go so far as to send him to the south of Italy and then abandon him to the wolves because things had backfired. He knew he would contact the PCS and that they would take his side and get him compensation. Someone would pay for this and it would not be him. He felt the anger seething in his gut and not only because the three men sitting on the other side of the meeting table had stabbed him in the back, but also because Layla had left him and was instigating divorce proceedings. The injustice of it all was astounding in its depth. How could Layla, she who had made his life an utter misery for the last twenty years, start divorce proceedings against him, citing unreasonable behaviour as grounds?

After the debacle at the villa in Afragola, Adam Standing and himself had been flown back to London on the early-morning flight the next day. A Metropolitan Police Service car had been waiting for them in Luton and had driven them straight to The Yard, where they were separated and interrogated for hours about the events, from when Thumper had been smacked in Roper's by Archie Moses.

After his interrogation, Detective Sergeant Thumper was told to report to the ACSO office at nine o'clock the next morning in full dress uniform. He knew what that meant. He would be the scapegoat for everything that had happened over the last couple of weeks.

Standing had been waiting in the car park out the back of The Yard when Thumper finally got out. "What happened?" he asked.

"They're going to stab me in the back," Dick had said, knowing it to be true.

He had almost resigned himself to it until he got the news about Layla. It was when he arrived at the flat in Peckham that he found the Royal Mail notice under the letter box to say that there was a registered letter waiting for him. He should have gone to bed and slept, but his mind was full of the coming dismissal and he knew he would not be able to sleep, so he had gone to the post office and collected the letter.

He opened it in the post office and was given some odd looks as he burst out in a guffaw. It was a notice from Layla's solicitor stating that she intended to begin divorce proceedings. He laughed because he had not even noticed that Layla was missing from the apartment. In fact, he had not thought about her since when he was in a cell in Pozzuoli nick, several days before.

Inspector Izzo lit a Gauloise as he walked away from the headquarters building in central Naples. He had been ordered to take a month's leave of absence, and that on his return he would be dismissed from the DIA and once again working as a State

Police Officer. It could have been worse, he mused, as a pulled a long drag from the cigarette. On his arrest, there had been much blustering about prosecution and dismissal from the service, but Izzo quickly gathered it was more to shut him up than a serious threat. Somehow, the ISS had decided that Izzo would very quickly deduce what had happened and rather than face that, they decided to let it rest. There was, however, no way the General or the Colonel would allow the circumvention of their authority to go unpunished. When they confronted Izzo, he intimated that a quiet life investigating ordinary street crime in Pozzuoli would the ideal end before he could retire peacefully as someone who had led a distinguished career. The General and the Colonel were instructed to let him move on from the DIA without any adverse comments on his record. The senior echelons did not want any news of the events to break into the current political landscape.

"Well?" Cipolle asked as he got into the car.

"I'm to take a vacation and then go back to being a policeman when I return."

Cipolle nodded. In truth, he had already known that Izzo was to be returned to the mundanity of enforcing speed limits, because the bosses had asked him to take over the role that Pietro's leaving the DIA would vacate. Cipolle might say that he felt sorry for the inspector, but that would not be true. All he felt was elation at the promotion. Now he would be able to conduct the investigations his way, a way that would be far better than his erstwhile boss's.

This time Archie did not opt for a Pro Bono lawyer. He had had enough of the legal system and wanted a lawyer who would resolve the issue in very quick order. He really did not want to take the chance of being assigned a kid just qualified and keen to make a name, knowing that such a kid would lack the tools to provide him with a viable defence. And he did not think he could stomach another do gooder like Alliss trying to get on the New Year's Honours list through pro bono work.

Not that he had been charged with anything yet. The Italians had extradited him back to the United Kingdom, because they said they did not want the paperwork that would be required to prosecute him. Archie knew, though, that they had sent him out of the country because they did not want him telling the world what he knew about the incident at the villa. The Italian media had already dubbed it Bagnoligate, and it was looking more and more like it was going to become something of a major constitutional crisis if not contained. During the current political turmoil, Italy could ill afford another scandal. They washed their hands of Archie because they could not be sure of what he knew, other than that he knew enough to tell stories about the Admiral being rescued by armed men in balaclavas under very strange circumstances, the signature uniform of the ISS.

"The Italians are not going to charge you with possession of a firearm, and I don't think that The Met can charge you with anything. They won't charge you with assaulting a police officer in Roper's, because that would still be exceedingly embarrassing for them."

"So, what does it all mean, then?"

"It means, Mr Moses, that as soon as I get your release sorted out, you can go back to being a celebrity bodyguard and try and forget the whole thing. Try and avoid hitting police officers in future, though. Not that you will see many bouncing in nightclubs for the foreseeable. The officer you assaulted in Roper's has been discharged from the service."

"Discharged for being assaulted?"

"No, he was discharged because moonlighting is considered gross misconduct."

Archie snorted. He guessed it would be regarded as common sense that having serving police officers bouncing in nightclubs should probably be avoided. Surely it is a conflict of interest? He thought. Well, what did he know, he was just a celebrity bodyguard.

He felt a little sympathy for Dick Thumper, who had been treated even more woefully. But as he walked out of The Yard, intent on returning to his life of overpaid babysitting for those with loads of money and no need of a babysitter. It was only a little sympathy, because, truth be told, Archie thought it was not his problem.